CRAVING A
YOUNG THUG'S

Part Two

A NOVEL BY

KALI JOE

"Well, thank you."

Anna placed the bag down on the table that contained the liquor and popped it open. I had one of my waitresses bring me three glasses so we could enjoy it.

"So Ronaysha, tell me what made you want to open such an extravagant place?" Anna asked, sipping her drink.

"I've always taken a liking to cooking since I was younger. I found a need in our area and met it. By the way, this alcohol is very good."

"Thank you," Stefano said, swooshing it around in his glass.

My cell started buzzing. I looked over at it to see Persian calling. I hit the ignore button and turned my attention back to Stefano and his wife, Anna. I was enjoying their company and from the sound of it, I had this deal in the bag. My phone was starting to become a distraction for all of us, so I turned it off.

"We know you are a very busy woman, Ronaysha, so before we leave, my wife and I would like to extend to you our business."

"Really? Oh my God, thank you so much!" I got up to shake their hands.

"Excuse me, Ronaysha, you have a call from Tank on line ten; he says it's an emergency," my manager interrupted.

"Please excuse me," I told Stefano as I picked up the phone.

"Nay, get your ass home right now. Don't ask questions right now. My mama just called me scared, so I'm on the way home too. Meet me there. NOW!" Tank said before hanging up.

"Is everything okay?" Anna asked.

"I'm sorry to end this, but I have an emergency at my home. I have to leave—please email me the documents and I will sign off on them," I told them as I gathered all my things.

"Please let us drive you," Anna suggested.

"No, I'll be fine," I shot over my shoulder, trying to hide my tears.

"Ronaysha, please let us take you. We can see that you're upset," Stefano stated.

Without fighting with them any longer, I slid into the car with them and told their driver where to go. Finally turning my phone back on, I saw several missed calls from Persian and Tank. I opened my purse to make sure I had my gun with me because my guts were doing flips. I kept glimpsing at Anna, but she seemed a bit uptight about something. I couldn't put my finger on it, though. I looked at Stefano squeeze her and she looked over at him. I looked out the window as we rounded the corner to my house. I reached in my purse and pulled out my gun, aiming it at Stefano and his wife.

"Who the fuck sent you?"

The unfazed look Stefano gave me sent chills up my spine. In my mind, I was thinking of ways to escape. I saw Anna try and slip something in my drink; instead of drinking it, I pretended to take a sip. I noticed that Stefano was someone I'd seen Kevin with when we first started dating. They thought they had me, but I was a made bitch straight from Orlando, Florida and if I was going to die, I was taking one of these bitches down with me.

"Nay, is that any way to treat an old friend?" Stefano said, smiling. I was a half of a second from my house, and I had a decision to make before we got there. I decided to take Anna out first because she appeared to be weak and scared. Sending a bullet through her skull, I then aimed my gun at Stefano.

"You're smarter than I thought you were, Nay. But see, this time Kevin outsmarted you," Stefano said as we pulled up to my house.

I was snatched by my shirt and dragged into my house, where I could hear the cries of my son coming from his room. T'Shay was lying on the floor in the foyer with half her face blown off. I became sick to my stomach seeing her like that. I bodied a few people myself, but T'Shay shared a special place in my heart, just like my mother. It was like reliving that day over again. Where were Tank and Persian when I needed them the most? I dropped my gun inside the car as I was dragged out. The sound of Stefano's expensive shoes could be heard on my marble floors. I tried to get up but he kicked me in the face, making me fall back. Blood spilled from my mouth as I spit out my two front teeth. He grabbed my shirt and punched me in my face like I was a grown man, making my eyes swell.

"Weak ass bitch," I managed to get out. "If you fuck with my son, I promise you I'll kill you with my bare hands."

I heard my son's cries getting closer. I wasn't able to really see who had my son because one of my eyes was closed shut and the other one was filled with blood. The person that was holding my son had on a rare perfume. It was a female. I continued to sniff her perfume. She briefly spoke in French before she walked out the door with my crying son. I tried with everything in me to get up and get my son, but Stefano hit me with his pistol and sent two shots to my chest.

I heard Stefano speaking in French as he made his way upstairs. He was obviously cursing in French because no one else was in the house but us. Stefano's dumb ass didn't even check to see if I was wearing a damn vest. I never got caught slipping without it, especially since I had my son. My chest was hurting, but I had to make a move before Stefano came back. Rolling over on my stomach so I could crawl to get the gun from under my table in the foyer, it was then that I realized my vision was blurred. I could only see objects once I was close up on them, but I knew my house like the back of my hand. The feeling of my body being snatched up and my mouth being covered frightened me.

"It's me ma, calm down," Tank whispered. "Here."

He handed me a Glock before he walked off and left me. It wasn't long before the sound of guns going off outside made Stefano run back down the stairs. This was my only shot to take this bitch out. I came from out of my hall closet, hoping that I could have enough sight to take him out. I closed my eye and when I opened them, Stefano was standing right in front of me, I smelled him. I aimed my gun and squeezed the trigger, emptying my clip into Stefano.

"Nay!" Tank's voice boomed throughout the house.

As tough as I was trying to be right now, I couldn't be; seeing Tank's face made me break down. His hands were empty, and he didn't have my baby.

"Where is he, Tank?" I cried out loud.

"I'm sorry ma, they left before I got here. Don't stress it, we gon' get him back," he kissed me.

He walked away and kneeled down by his mama. I could see the tears falling from his face.

"Fuck niggas want war with a young thug! They killed my muthafuckin' mama, Nay! My gotdamn mama!" Tank screamed. "I'm killing every fucking body until I get my son back and avenge my mama's death," he said to no one in particular.

I cocked my nine, "Let's get our muthafuckin' son back."

Nay

I hadn't had time to get my mind right before I called an emergency meeting. I sat at the head of the table between Persian and Tank with one bloodshot eye, and the other one closed shut. I wasn't concerned with my appearance, but what I was concerned with was who had my son. Everyone that sat around the table was so worried about me, and really they should be, because Kevin had brought out the real bitch in me. In front of me sat the gun that I killed Stefano with. I reloaded it and was ready to use it at any time. Kevin had betrayed me for the last time, and I was wanting his blood. I called this meeting, but I really didn't know what I wanted to say. Persian looked over at me and gripped my hand as he cleared his throat.

"Y'all, things just got real," Persian cleared his throat again trying to fight back his tears. "My nephew is missing right now. All we know is it's a female that has him. I want y'all to go to anybody associated with Kevin's pussy ass and kill 'em. I want my nephew back in my sister's hands as soon as possible, and if everybody got to die, then so muthafuckin' be it. There will be no dope moving in the city until he's safe, so nobody eats. Period! Get out there and make it happen."

Persian got up from his chair, knocking it down with a loud bang. Tank got up and went behind him. Everyone piled out of the warehouse except Breya and Dre. Breya sat in the chair that Tank got up from and grabbed me, placing my head on her chest. I wanted to cry, I just couldn't. I had gotten so damn comfortable thinking everything between Kevin was cool.

"We gon' get nephew back, Nay. You already know I'm riding, pregnant and all, fuck it," Breya exclaimed.

All I could do was shake my head. My voice was lost. I didn't know what to do. I felt like a lost child in the middle of an amusement park without my son. My breasts were swelling because I hadn't pumped or put him on my breasts today. All I could think about was, was he eating? Was he crying? Whoever had him, I hoped the bitch hadn't brought any harm to him when I found him.

"Come on so we can get you checked out," Persian announced.

We all went our separate ways. Persian drove as Tank rested his head on my chest. We both were hurting. I knew exactly how he felt to come in and see his mother dead.

"Persian, take us home. I'll ice my eye. I don't feel like explaining shit to the police right now," I told him.

He glared at me through the rearview mirror. "They already fucking involved. We got a missing baby and a dead body at your house. We can't just hide the fact your neighbors seen all that shit pop off. Thankfully, I handled the shit with one of the detectives on the scene. You still got to go holla at them just to say you showed your face; all the other shit handled."

"Just take us to a room, bruh," Tank suggested.

Persian headed towards some hotels that were close to his house. I wasn't in the mood to talk to anyone. I rubbed Tank's head as I looked out the windows. Finally, the tears started falling. I was the type of female that was in control of everything. I felt like I was losing control.

My son was depending on me and I couldn't even protect him. I quickly wiped my face as Persian pulled into the Omni.

"Y'all sit tight, I'll pay for it. Damn sure don't want you going in looking like that, Nay," Persian said, getting out the car.

Tank raised his head up and kissed my lips. I don't know how we were going to get through this, but we both needed each other. He had to bury his mother all the while combing the streets looking for our son, Prince. Ten minutes later, Persian came out with our room keys and we were on our way. Persian made me put his hoodie on and cover my face. He was on high alert right now and he felt like Kevin wasn't going to be satisfied until he offed all of us. He thought the more I stayed hidden, the better. Before he left, he made me promise to let everyone else handle this while I stayed put. I promised, but shit, who was I fooling? My damn self.

I walked in the bathroom and turned the shower on for Tank and I. I finally looked at myself in the mirror. I took my finger and lifted my top lip. My two front teeth were completely gone; the area where they were was swollen. I couldn't help but to cry, looking at myself. My eye was shut closed and the other one was red. I took a hard swallow as I put my head down. I stripped out of my clothes and stepped in the shower. As the water hit me, I thought about how I slipped today. I let my son down knowing his father was a snake. As I washed my body with the hotel soap, the scent of the woman hit my nose again. It wasn't an expensive perfume but it wasn't cheap either. She spoke French, but she sounded nothing like Stefano and his dead bitch Anna. I rinsed off and turned the water off since Tank never got in.

Entering the room, I saw Tank sitting in the chair, staring out the patio window at the city of Orlando. It was beautiful, and just to think that my son was out there somewhere frustrated me.

"Get some rest, baby. I'm taking you to get your mouth fixed in the morning. We got a lot of shit to do tomorrow. I got you some ice, too, so put some ice on your eye to keep it from swelling. I don't need muthafuckas thinking I'm putting my damn hands on you," he spoke. He never turned around to look at me and that bothered me. I knew right now I wasn't much to look at but damn, I was already feeling like shit.

I hung the towel up, turned the lights off, and slipped into bed. I knew I wasn't going to sleep, but at least lying down would help me. It only made my thoughts run faster.

***

I kept checking on Tank throughout the night, and he never moved from that spot, not even to piss. He just sat there stoned faced until it was almost scary. It was now eight in the morning and he was just getting out the shower. He still carried the same look on his face. He had already told me my appointment was at nine so I was up, getting myself ready.

"Tank, are we going to be okay?" I asked him. I was unsure if our fresh relationship was going to last. He had just turned twenty and I had a birthday coming up in a few months.

"What you mean? Yea we gon' be okay," he told me.

"I mean us, Tank. Like me and you?"

"Man, Nay, don't start this shit right now, okay?" He dried off and put his clothes on.

After he was dressed and ready to go, he grabbed my face and kissed my lips.

"You still sexy as fuck even while you snag tooth. Bring your ass on because I got shit to do," Tank said.

He was still rude as hell. He didn't care anything about my feelings right now. Just knowing he loved me regardless made me feel a little better.

Tank

Nay squeezed my hand as they lowered my mama in the ground. A nigga would be lying if I said I wasn't hurting. My damn mama was my best friend; shit, she was all I had since my ole man was old as dirt. I looked over at him sitting in the wheelchair with his dark shades on his face. His hands violently shook as he wiped his face. His nurse stood behind him, rubbing his back. My ole man was still fresh as hell. He wore his Tom Ford shoes even though he could barely walk. His suit was crisp and his salt and pepper hair was freshly cut. My mama always made sure he was straight. I guess it was all on me now.

Once she was lowered, they started throwing the dirt on her pretty pearl and diamond casket. I got up and threw my ivory rose in there with her so she would know I would always be there. I grabbed Nay's hand and approached my ole man. I eyed the nurse and she already knew to give me some privacy.

"Pops, this my lady, Nay."

He took his shades off and revealed his blueish gray eyes. He was still handsome and that's why my mama fell in love with him. Well, she also told me he had a mini man hanging between his legs, but shit, I didn't want to know that. That shit made me sick to my stomach just thinking about it.

"Nice to meet you, Nay. I'm Rowe, this nigga's daddy." He smiled at Nay showing his nice white dentures.

"Nice to meet you," Nay said.

"Pops, I know Mama gone, but you know I got you regardless. I'm only a call away and I'll try to get to you at least once a week."

"Shit, I ain't got to wait on your ass to do shit for me, son. I'm old, but I ain't dumb and your mama ain't either; she made sure I was gon' be straight. We all know the life we live. Shit, we don't know when we gon' leave this bitch. I'm surprise a bitch ass nigga ain't caught my old ass slipping yet," he chuckled.

"I know you straight, Pops, but I'm just letting you know I'm here," I reassured him.

"Alright, son. Damn, I'm gon' miss T'shay's crazy ass. That woman there was a piece of damn work, I swear," he said.

"I know, but now she lives in my crazy ass."

"Hell yea," he said, coughing.

His nurse came running over with his oxygen mask and placed it on his face. His COPD was getting the best of him. I took his weak hand in mine and squeezed it, before bending down to hug him and tell him I love him. Hearing him say it back always made me feel better. I got picked at because my mama fucked the old man from the block. What they didn't know about my daddy was he ran numbers and had plenty of money, but he never flexed his money until my mama started dressing him. His nurse flashed us a smile and rolled him to the car. I was surprised to see Persian hadn't left, but I knew as long as Nay was out here he wasn't going anywhere.

"Y'all straight?" Persian asked.

"We good, bruh," I told him.

"Well, I'm about to head out and check on a few things. Hit me up so we can link up later, Tank."

"I got you.

We dapped and hugged. He then pulled Nay and hugged her tight, placing a kiss on her forehead.

"Soon," he whispered in her ear.

We were going on a week since Prince had been gone. Nobody in Orlando knew anything. We went through Kevin's hood and cleared that bitch out, but still came up empty-handed. I couldn't stand seeing my baby looking depressed. A nigga was doing all he could, but I was starting to feel like it wasn't enough. Nay even voiced this week that if we kept coming up empty-handed, she was going to make something happen. I wasn't sure what her something was, so I stayed out all night trying to come up with something. I was damn near sleep deprived, but I would never tell her that.

The limo pulled back up to our two-bedroom condo. I hated this little ass shit Nay picked out, but I didn't want to argue with her, so I settled for this little shit. I felt like I was suffocating and I was trying not to show Nay, but right now, I wasn't in the fucking mood to be in the damn house. I hadn't been doing anything but combing the streets looking for my son while she sat her ass in the house with all that got damn crying. I couldn't touch her or anything.

I walked in our room and changed out of my suit and put on a pair of grey sweatpants and a white t-shirt along with a pair of Air Max. I looked at myself in the mirror before I grabbed the keys to my car.

"Where the fuck you going?" Nay gave me attitude.

"Out," I said over my back.

"Tank, don't walk your ass out that got damn door," Nay yelled.

I turned the knob and walked right out that bitch. It wasn't nothing against her, it was just I needed to breath; get high and drunk just to clear my head. I saw my mama's head blown off and I still hadn't grieved like I should. I loved the fuck out of Nay but shit, I needed to do me. My phone started ringing before I could even get in my car.

"Nay, stop all that damn hollering. I'll be back in a few hours, shit," I hung the phone in her face. That pussy Stefano fucked her face up a little and she was being insecure about it. Her ass was still fine as fuck to me. I replaced her damn teeth and she was still acting like they were missing. I pulled into traffic. I planned to go hang with my uncle Peedie; he always had the good weed.

Nay

ubbing my tongue across my brand new front teeth that I was still adjusting to, I watched Deedra maneuver back and forth from her car. I took a pull from my blunt as I looked at her face. No one had seen her since my sister-in-law rearranged her face. She had to go through extensive surgery because she had so many broken bones in her face. She wore her weaves over her left eye now because she had an artificial eye. I still didn't trust this bitch though. Tank and Persian were going around killing all these people, but my gut was telling me they were barking up the wrong tree. I'd been following this bitch for four days in my rental. She was still carrying bags in her brand new apartment. The bitch moved, got a new car and everything. I don't know if it was from being happy or from nobody fucking with her, but the bitch was huge now.

Adjusting my ball cap on my head, I placed my shades on as I approached her. Before she could close her door, I pushed the door back open, startling her. She pulled her hair from her eye to get a good look at me like she could really see out of her fake eye. I stood there with my gun in my hand. I pushed my way into her house with my six-inch heels clacking against her new hardwood floors. Her little spot was nice, definitely better than her last piece of shit apartment.

"Nay," she said above a whisper.

"Where my got damn baby at, Deedra?"

"I don't have your baby, Nay. I promise I don't," she cried.

"You still fucking with Kevin so I know you know what's going on, bitch," I spat.

"Nay, I promise you I haven't fucked with Kevin in a minute. Look at me! Who the fuck wants me looking so hideous," she explained.

I took in her appearance and cringed. Her lip had a small droop to it. Her jaw was sunk in and she had several scars on her face. A part of me felt bad for her but shit, you can't go around putting niggas' dicks in your mouth and thinking nobody's gon' whoop your ass.

I brushed past her as I looked around her house. She had no sign of my baby anywhere.

"You happy now?" she asked with tears in her eyes.

"Don't fuck with me right now, Deedra. If you speak to Kevin, you tell that pussy ass nigga that I won't rest until I can smell his blood running out his neck," I told her.

I looked at her ass one last time before I headed towards my car with my phone ringing. I looked at it and rolled my eyes. This relationship with Tank was draining the shit out of me. Yes, I loved his young ass, but I didn't like the fact that he could come and go as he wanted but I had to sit still. If it was up to me, I would have my damn baby back by now. I got in the car and pulled off. I couldn't even make it to the stop sign before it was ringing again.

"What is it, Tank?"

"Nay, where the hell you at? The muthafuckin' streets hot and you got your black ass out in the streets. Get your ass here now!" Tanked screamed in the phone.

"Fuck you, Tank. Did you not just stay your ass out all night last night? Get the fuck off my line, bitch," I spat before hanging up.

I made a quick turn heading towards my shoe store. Since I was out, I might as well do something I wanted to do. Working at home was getting boring, so going into the store would possibly make me feel better. I then had a plan to stop by Queen and Prince and see how that was running as well. I had beefed up security ever since the accident with Stefano last week.

"Ronaysha, what are you doing here? Surely you should be home resting," one of my employees stated.

"I'm fine. If I stay in the house any longer there's no telling what I would do." I set my purse down and put my code in to check the registers. Smiling, I closed everything up and headed to my office. It felt good to sit in my chair. I was so focused on the restaurant that I let my shoe store slip. I stopped coming by as much and just trusted my staff to do their job.

I powered on my computer so I could browse for some new shoes for the season when my door got kicked in.

"Didn't I tell you to bring your ass home?" Tank stood over me fuming.

I didn't budge as I kept scrolling the internet. My computer went crashing to the floor, busting the screen once it made contact with the floor. I still didn't react. I pushed my chair back and walked around Tank to grab my purse. I refused to get into it with him in my place of business, but once I made it home, I was giving this bastard the business.

"Nay, bring your ass back here," he yelled at me.

"Y'all call me if you need me," I encouraged my staff.

I pushed the door open and swiftly walked to my rental. I hit the unlock button and tried to climb in but was blocked.

"You one stubborn ass muthafucka. When I tell your ass to do something that's what you need to do. While you out here running your ass around, you got a price on your got damn head that would make a crackhead try to kill you. Get your ass in the damn car."

I tried to get in the rental but he snatched me out of it.

"Nah, not this damn car. My damn car. Aye, Whizz, come take this shit back to wherever it belongs," Tank barked.

I snatched my arm away from him and walked towards his car and climbed in. He looked over at me as he talked to the dude taking the car. I pulled my phone out and sent Breya a text so I could see what was going on. Who the fuck got a price on my head? I put my phone in my purse as Tank got in the car and stared at me.

"Fuck is your problem, Nay? You got a nigga out here aggressive because your ass won't listen," Tank stated.

"Who got a price on my head?" I asked. That's all I was worried about at this point. If I got caught slipping I would never see my son again.

Tank started the car and headed home without answering me. We made it home and he still had yet to give me an answer.

"Tank, I can't do this shit with you. I can tell you ain't really fucking with me like that so you can leave or I can leave," I told him.

"I ain't going no fucking where. I'm pissed off with your ass, Nay. Take that shit like a fucking woman. I ain't no controlling ass nigga, but when I tell you to come home, that's what the fuck I mean, you understand me?"

"No, I don't fucking understand you, Tank. Don't forget that I can hold my fucking own in the streets. If you and Persian stop with the fucking hiding shit from me, I could better know how to handle myself. So fuck all that you screaming," I spazzed.

"Fuck all that I'm talking about? Huh? Okay, so you wanna know what's up, huh? Feast your eyes on this shit right here," he hit me in the face with a balled-up piece of paper.

I opened and read it. I couldn't help but cry while reading it. The amount of money made my heartbeat speed up. This shit was real and I was playing. I looked up at Tank as he wiped my tears from my eyes.

"Fuck that nigga, Nay. Listen to me when I say I got you. I can't get to that nigga from the inside because he got a squad around him. I need you to stay fucking put unless push comes to shove. We got to get the fuck out of Orlando too."

"I can't leave just in case my baby is still here," I whined.

"Nay, we got to get out of here. We won't be far but just enough outside the city. Go lie down and rest. I'll be back with some food," Tank said, softly kissing me.

I waited until Tank was out the door before I started looking for a flight to Miami. Kevin had been begging me to see him and that's just what I was going to do. I knew money changed people but I never would've thought Kevin would bite the hand that fed his ass. I didn't have a clue how I was going to get away from Tank and Persian, but I was planning on making a move within a week. It was time for me to get my shit together. I was tired of playing the weak victim; now I was about to be the victimizer, and the first bitch I was going to see was his mama.

***

Pussy sore the next morning, I got up and showered as I lounged around until Tank decided to leave. I ordered an Uber and headed to this pussy nigga's mama house. Nothing had changed in the neighborhood. Same mangy ass dogs in the yard. The paint was still peeling off the house and you could barely get on her porch because all the damn plants this bitch had. I covered my nose and mouth as I rang the doorbell. I knew the smell of a dead body. The flies were forming at the base of the door. Maggots were forming as well. I grabbed my shirt and opened the door. I gagged as the door opened. I walked through the house and sure enough, the old bitch was dead. I stepped over her decayed body and checked her mail. I stepped back over her, going towards the door.

"Burn in hell, bitch!"

Bitch never liked me. She let Kevin lay up in her house with hoes all the time, and when I would come over, she would act like he wasn't home. She would sit there and curse me out if I even attempted to leave her son. She dogged me out behind my back and even caused Kevin to slap the shit out of me in front of one his hoes because she lied and said I disrespected her.

I pulled my phone out to call the police then thought about it.

22

"Fuck that hoe," I said as I got back in the Uber and headed home.

On the way home, I wondered why Kevin hadn't at least sent someone to check on his mom or anything. I knew him and his mom were close so now my mind was running a mile a minute trying to figure out what Kevin had up his sleeve. I looked down at my hands and noticed I didn't have on any gloves.

"Shit!" I yelled.

"Are you okay, ma'am?" the driver asked, looking in the mirror.

"I'm fine," I replied.

Tank was going to kill me. I had a choice to go back later and burn that bitch down or take my chances at telling Tank what the fuck I did today.

Kevin

*L*ooking at my phone, it was almost time for my meet up. I tied my long dreads to the back of my head and checked myself out in the mirror. I was what every female correctional officer wanted. Shit, to be honest, I haven't met a female yet that didn't want me. I was light skinned with light grey eyes, tall, and my swag stayed on point. I'll talk any bitch out of their drawers. I didn't give a fuck about a bitch, not even my mama. That's why I let her ass rot in her house even after Persian came and told me he murked her. Yea, I was mad because it was a low blow, but fuck her too. I did have love for her until I landed in here and she cut me off. My mama kept all my shit and snorted it up her got damn nose. She better be glad Persian got to her before I did because it would've been worse.

I looked at my roommate as he wrote some urban book shit. Nobody was going to want his dumb ass book. I got tired of hearing the nigga talk about it. The nigga stuttered so hard I often wondered how his writing looked. I walked out into the hallway and made my way down to my meeting spot. Most of the men were gambling or minding their business. I ran Miami, so most of the inmates were eating in here because of me. I guess you're wondering how I went from being with Nay and having nothing, to having a little something. I was with Nay for years. Shit, she basically put me on and showed me how to make money. Persian was against even bringing me in, but he pretty much melts when Nay ask for anything. All the money I was making with them, I eventually established my own connect. I had money stashed everywhere. Deedra had some, but she fucked it up. My mama had some, but she fucked it up as well. I had two more bitches that I had holding for me and one was standing right in front of me with her uniform already off.

"Hey, baby," she smiled, walking towards me.

I slapped her on her ass as she started taking off my clothes. I met up with her at least three times a week. She wrapped her mouth around my dick and handled her business. After I nutted down her throat, I bent her ass over a stack of boxes in the inventory closet. Her pussy was trash but a nigga had to do something in this bitch. I closed my eyes and thought about Nay so I could catch my nut. I don't know why I always thought about Nay when I fucked these bitches, but it always helped make the process better. I yanked out of her and sprayed my nut all over her back. She had to work twelve hours with my nut on her, but I didn't really give a fuck. I got her shirt off the floor and wiped myself off.

"Really, Kevin?" she snatched it from me.

"You know I don't like leaving your juices on me," I told her as I shrugged. "How my baby doing?"

"He's doing good. Are you sure she's not going to find me?"

I walked up to her and grabbed her face softly. "The only way she's going to know is if you run your mouth. No one else knows but you and Stefano. We know he's not going to talk now that he's dead. Now get back to work so you can continue to take care of my son."

She placed a kiss on my cheek and handed me a bag of pills. That's why I fucked with her heavy. Not only was she Stefano's niece, but she only started working here just for me. She brought in everything I needed and I gave her the money that I made to put up. She wasn't scared of anything except for Ronaysha Maxwell. I stuffed the pills under my nuts and walked out, leaving her there to get her juices off of her shirt.

I walked out into population and ran straight into another female CO I was sleeping with. If she sees Syriah come out of the closet, all hell was going to break loose.

"What you doing in there, Kevin?" She looked me up and down and looked around me to see who would come out the closet.

"Don't do this shit right here, Lacy."

"Don't do what? Don't forget I got the damn uniform on, Kevin. Who in the closet?"

I attempted to walk away, hoping Lacy would follow me. Once she heard the closet door pop open, she turned around to look Syriah in her face. Syriah was black and Italian so her olive skin turned red instantly.

"You've got to be kidding," Lacy laughed. "This dumb bitch, Kevin, really? You've just cost this bitch her job."

I yanked Lacy by her shirt and dragged her in the same closet I had Syriah in and locked the door. I could do shit like this here because I paid some of the male COs more than they got paid to wear them funky ass uniforms. Lacy stared at me with her arms across her chest. She was spoiled, but she had every reason to be; she was really the love of my life. Being from Miami, Lacy was my first girlfriend. All the times I flew back home to Miami, I lied to Nay, telling her I was coming to check on my grandmother, when I was really out here with Lacy. I enjoyed being with Lacy, but she just wasn't enough to make a nigga settle down. She had no idea about Nay and my son, and I wanted to keep it that way.

"Lacy, don't make that girl lose her job. Get your damn feelings in check," I told her.

"So you really think it's okay to just fuck my co-worker, Kevin? That's not fucking cool," she cried.

I walked up to her and wrapped her in my arms. I started kissing her neck. Once I heard her moan, I knew I had her. I lifted her head and kissed her lips, as I unfastened her uniform shirt. It didn't take long for my dick to spring back to life. These women were so damn dumb. Fuck one bitch raw and go into the next bitch. I guess that's why Nay and I never got along because she was so damn bull headed and it was only so much she was going to let a nigga do. Lacy broke our kiss and dropped down to her knees, removed the pills, and took all nine inches of my dick in her mouth. Nasty bitch slurping on another bitch juices. I moved her bob to the side so I could watch her enjoy the taste. I bit down on my lips and closed my eyes again, imagining Nay was on her knees with that fat ass bouncing as she gave me head.

"That's it, Nay. Suck that shit," I grunted.

"Who the fuck is Nay?" Lacy looked up at me with my now limp dick in her hand.

"Lacy, what the fuck you talking 'bout?"

"You just called me Nay, nigga. Who is that?"

"You just hearing shit," I told her as I fixed my clothes. "You got my dick limp then a muthafucka. Don't fuck with me for the rest of day."

"I'm sorry, Kevin. I could've sworn I heard you say Nay," she whined.

I looked her ass up and down, and then walked out the door. She heard me right; I did call my baby mama's name. I couldn't get that bitch off my brain. The only way to do it was to kill her.

Tank

*C*lenching my jaws, I watched Nay dry off. The call I just received from Persian pissed me off, and she was my target. I was distracted by her body but this was business first, and then I'd fuck the shit out of her to punish her. She slipped her legs into her lace underwear and pulled one of my white wife beaters out of my drawer and placed it over her head. It barely covered her double-D breasts.

"Nay, what you did yesterday?" I eyed her.

"Nothing, I stayed in the house. That's all you let me do," she rolled her eyes.

I pulled from my blunt and watched her intently. I could tell she was nervous by the way she was fidgeting around the room.

"You sure you didn't leave the house yesterday a little after three?"

"No, Tank, damn."

"I can't stand a lying muthafucka and that's exactly what you are right now." I raised up out of the chair I was sitting in and approached her.

"Tank, go on now. I'm not in the mood for your shit today," she attempted to push me away.

"Because your fat ass want to be hardheaded, I should let the got damn homicide detective lock your ass up for leaving all them prints in Kevin mama's house. You still want to lie to a nigga?" I backed her into the dresser.

"Okay, damn! Yes, I went over there because I thought the bitch had my baby. I knew I fucked up once I left out the bitch house," she confessed.

"Why the fuck you didn't say anything, Nay, damn? You got the muthafuckin' pigs over there. Good thing your brother is connected because you would be fucked. I don't know what I'm going to do with your hardheaded ass. If your pussy wasn't good I would've been left your ass. Take this shit off so I can taste it," I said, pulling at her lace panties.

We both had a lot of tension to get off. I had to fuck this shit out of her because I was leaving town for about two weeks. I picked her up and placed her on the chair I was just sitting in. I opened her thick thighs and buried my face in between her legs. It didn't take long for her to wet my beard up. I sucked and kissed softly on her clit until I brought her to another orgasm. I raised up and took my basketball shorts and boxers off. With her juices still on my lips, I kissed her so she could taste herself. We let our tongues play tag as I entered her tight hole. The popping sound her pussy made every time I pulled my rod out made my dick swell. I pulled my dick out and slapped it on her clit, making her squirt.

"Flip over," I demanded.

Once she flipped over, I pushed down in her back to get that perfect arch. Seeing her cream on my dick was all I needed to release my seed in her. I fell on top of her, trying to catch my breath. My heart was racing from the nut I just received. My dick finally went limp and slipped out of her. I got up and went to the bathroom and came back with a warm washcloth to clean her up.

"Nay, I got to go out of town for a few weeks."

"What the fuck, Tank? You can't do this right now. My son is damn missing and you talking about going out of town. Where the hell you going?" she sat up in the chair.

"I'm going to meet your uncle Lou."

"You going way to another damn country, Tank? I'm sure he would come here. Persian put you up to this shit?"

"No, Nay. He hit me up and told me I needed to see him immediately. I'm not fucking with your uncle like that so I'm leaving tonight."

"Tonight?!" Nay yelled. "Well I'm going too," she got up to start packing.

"No hell you ain't. You gon' keep your monkey ass here just in case something pops off," I commanded.

She got up and walked out the room. I didn't have time to chase behind her right now. I had shit to do and a long ass flight to catch. Persian told me not to be cocky with their uncle Lou. He was the provider of all their drugs and I didn't need to go and fuck anything up. I didn't want to leave Nay but shit had to be done.

***

My flight to Colombia was long and rough. A nigga was tired as shit. I wanted to sleep, but Uncle Louie wanted to meet with me as soon as I landed. When I walked through the airport, there was a Spanish man waiting for me with my name on a card. I walked up to him and introduced myself in Spanish. I guess he was a little shocked to see a young nigga speak in his language. He escorted me to a car. Uncle Lou pulled out all the stops with the personal driver. He had some of the best weed rolled I'd ever smoked. Pulling up to a massive mansion, I sat up and looked as several armed men walked up to the car. Clearing the driver to enter, we pulled up in front of Uncle Lou's estate.

"He's clear, guys," Uncle Lou stated as the guys patted me down as soon as I got out of the car.

They released me and I walked up to Uncle Lou. We talked a few times on the phone and I could tell he had trust issues, especially with new men. He looked me over closely as I approached. Being a young nigga from Orlando, I wasn't dressed in a damn suit. Shit, I had on some Nike jogging pants and a white t-shirt with a pair of all white Air Max.

"Talik, it's a pleasure," he held his massive hand for me to shake it. When I placed my hand in his, he snatched me towards him. "Don't fuck with me. My niece and nephew vouched for your young ass. Don't say nothing that's going to piss me off," he said in my ear.

I looked him in his eyes and shook my head.

"Good. Follow me," he led the way into the house.

My eyes almost popped out of my head as I watched the half-naked women walking around the house catering to him. This nigga was living like Hugh Heffner. It was going to be a long ass week. I wasn't trying to fuck none of these Spanish bitches, they were crazy as hell. Coming down the stairs was the most beautiful woman I'd seen since laying eyes on Nay.

"This must be Nay's boyfriend," she eyed me.

"Yes, and I want you to keep your fast ass away from him. If I even find out you're sniffing his dick, I'm going to cut you up and send you back to your mama," Uncle Lou told her.

Now I saw where Persian and Nay got their savage from. She looked me over again before sashaying away. I couldn't help but look at her ass. But her belly button told on her; her body was as fake as a damn plastic Barbie.

"Stay the fuck away from her. That's my daughter, Camellia. She's very fucking dangerous with her mouth. Bitch don't care who she put her mouth on. I found her eating my damn wife out and she didn't care that I caught her. I should've killed her then but her mama begged me not too. She got one more time and I'm sending her back to her poor ass mama in Cuba."

I ran my hand over my waves. I had to get my damn mind right. I couldn't let this little bitch get me off. I did want to know what that mouth do though.

#

I had to admit I was fine as fuck. Since my son has been gone, I lost about ten pounds; but I needed to lose it. Jumping my big ass in my jeans, I laid on the bed to fasten them. If I could give some ass away, I surely would. Tank was crazy about my ass, but he didn't know what it felt like to carry this shit around behind me. I pulled my Balmain black suede shoes out the box and put them on my feet. I checked my black clutch to make sure I had everything I needed inside. Taking my wave cap off, I brushed my waves and walked out the door.

"Ms. Maxwell, will you be out for an extended time?" the bellhop asked.

"It will be a while," I replied.

He helped me in the car and I pulled off. I let the top back to my new car so the breeze could hit me. It was beautiful out today and I was feeling myself. Taking the long ass drive from Biscayne Bay to the federal prison gave me time to get all my thoughts together. It's been months since I'd seen Kevin. My heart was cold for him and if I could kill him today, I would. He wasn't expecting to see me today. Knowing his dumb ass, he hadn't changed his paperwork so I knew my name was still on his visitation list.

I let the top up before I pulled into the parking garage. I watched as all the lame bitches came to see these sorry ass niggas that was selling them fake ass dreams about when they get out. I grabbed my stuff and got out of the car. I got a few eye rolls but I was used to that shit. The female CO was giving me a hard time about coming to see him. I knew he was fucking a few of them but that didn't have shit to do with me. I didn't want the nigga; I was just coming to get some shit clear. I watched the girl shuffle through some paperwork as I admired my nails. I knew she was about to be on some bullshit so I prepared my mouth.

"What you said your name was again?" she looked at me.

"Ronaysha Maxwell," I replied.

"Umm, yea. I don't see your name on his paperwork," she said.

I looked at her name on her shirt and it read CO Romono. I calmly got my words together as I placed my clutch down.

"Ms. Romono, I know for a fact my name is on his paperwork. Now, if you need to call your supervisor down here to help you look, then you need to do that because I'm not leaving."

She popped her lips and walked off leaving a long line of people waiting. He was most definitely sleeping with that hoe because she was adamant about not letting me see him. She was his type as well, with her rare breed ass. She started walking back towards me with another female that had a scowl on her face.

"What's the problem?" the other officer asked.

"Excuse me, what's your name?" I inquired.

"You wanted a supervisor, right?"

"Well damn, who pissed in your damn cereal? I'm being polite. Could you check inmate Kevin Highsmith's paperwork and see if I'm on there for visitation," I told her.

She shuffled through some papers and rolled her eyes at me. Now looking at her, she was not Kevin's type so I don't know what her deal was today. She handed me my license back and let me through. I sashayed through the visitation table trying to find a spot to sit that was private. From the looks of it, there was no privacy. I sat down and waited for him to come out. These niggas did what the fuck they wanted to do in here. I could clearly see a bitch getting fingered while she jacked a nigga off. Thirsty ass thots would take the chance of getting caught to keep their nigga happy.

"Oh shit!"

I rolled my eyes at the sound of his voice. I gripped my purse tightly, wishing I could've brought my shit in here to end his life. I waited for him to get to my table. He sat down, throwing his long dreads over his shoulders. His once beautiful grey eyes were cold to me now.

"What brings my fine ass baby mama here to see me?" he asked, licking his lips. That once made me moist in the panties but the way Tank's young ass was handling my shit, I don't think Kevin would ever be able to get me wet again.

"You know why the fuck I'm here, Kevin. The only thing keeping me from killing your ass is this musky ass prison," I said, frowning.

"Nay, you ain't gon' do shit. How's my son? I know you didn't bring your fine ass all the way here to argue with me," he chuckled.

"Bitch, don't ask me how my son doing. I need to be asking your dick in the booty ass how he doing since you're the one that kidnapped him."

The look on his face said it all.

"I wouldn't harm my son, Nay," he leaned back.

"Is this coming from the same man that sent muthafuckas to kill me while I was pregnant? Get the fuck out of here. I came here to let you know I'm on your ass, Kevin. Even if I have to kill every bitch that's connected to you, I will. You know personally not to fuck with me. The only reason I was soft on your ass was because I loved you, but I don't anymore, so just know I'll kill you too, bitch," I told him.

"Nay, don't play that tough shit with me. That little fuck boy you fucking with got you sounding real damn big, but you ain't shit and never will be. Yea, I got my muthafuckin' son and you'll never see him again with your dumb ass," Kevin told me.

I'd had enough of his shit. I reached across the table and grabbed him by his dreads and slammed his head down on the table, cracking his nose. My rage got the best of me because I picked his head up and slammed it down again before some officers came to grab me. My shoes were flying across the room and my titties were now out. I was pissed knowing he had my son and wouldn't tell me where he was. Kevin managed to get a smirk off with blood dripping down his face. The same bitch that was giving me a hard time came to tend to him and take him to the back. I was handcuffed and taken to the back to be escorted to Dade County Jail. This other bitch was babysitting me with her exotic ass. She didn't even look like she needed to be working here.

"Fuck you keep staring at, hoe?" I asked her.

"Pipe that shit down. I'm not your baby daddy, bitch. You handcuffed and it's only me and you in this bitch. I'll beat your big ass and act like you got damn fell, hoe," she threatened.

"Uncuff me and try that shit with your ugly ass. Yea, like I thought. Get me the fuck out of here and take me to jail so I can post bail."

Breya

I didn't know what kind of shit Nay had done got herself into, but I was flying down the highway trying to get to her. It was going to take me three hours but the way traffic was flowing, I would make it in two hours and a half. I know I needed to get to her before Persian or Tank heard about her being in jail. I swerved in and out of traffic as I explained to Dre that I would be careful. Things were going good for us and the kids. Blake was still on her bullshit, but as soon as I had this baby, I was going to put that bitch in the dirt. I was developing a close relationship with Shay since she was the only girl. Nico and Dash were always giving her hell, so I spent most of my time with her. I made sure she got her hair done, nails done, and got her some clothes. I was pissed that I saw how much money Blake made in a night and she couldn't take care of the kids. Not to mention the amount of money Dre was giving her ass.

After stopping to piss several times, I finally made it to Dade County Police Department. I wasn't worried about the cash I paid to get Nay's ass out of jail. I was more concerned with her wellbeing and why the fuck she was down here seeing Kevin's ass. I signed my name on the paperwork and sat down to wait.

"Shit," I said as Persian's name popped up on my phone. I fumbled to answer it.

"Bre! Where you at? I need you to do something for me," Persian spoke into the phone.

"I'm kinda caught up doing something," I partially lied.

"Fuck you at? Nay's muthafuckin' ass is nowhere to be found. Did y'all forget we got shit to do round this bitch?" he fussed.

"No, Persian. I'll be there in a few," I hung up as Nay walked through the doors.

"Bitch, what the fuck you doing way down here? Persian spazzing the fuck out 'cause we not in place."

"Can I at least walk out this nasty piece of shit before you start all that damn nagging," Nay replied.

I already had a blunt rolled because I knew she was going to need it. Her motherly duties kicked in quick and she looked down at my stomach right before she lit the blunt.

"Let's get a room. I got a lot of shit to tell you and I really need this damn blunt, but I'm not about to smoke it around your pregnant ass."

After checking into a room, I let Nay take a shower and smoke before I questioned her again. With her eyes low, she sat on the other bed and cried. I got up and grabbed her.

"He got my son, Breya," she was able to say through her cries.

"Before we leave Miami, we will have him back. Wipe them got damn tears and let's start planning. We got about forty-eight hours before Persian really gets on our ass. You need to find out who the fuck he knows down here; what bitch he fucking and we'll kill they ass until we get answers," I told Nay.

***

Nay told me about the two bitches giving her a hard time down at the prison. The one we wanted first was this little mixed breed bitch that had so much to say while Nay was cuffed. Evidently, the hoe was off today because she hadn't left her house since we followed her here after her shift last night. I looked over at Nay as she avoided answering Tank's call. We both were in some deep shit, so we might as well go out with a bang.

"Look at this shit," I said.

Nay looked up. I could feel the heat radiating off her body. Pulling the gun from her holster under her pants leg, she put one in the chamber.

"Hold on," I grabbed her arm.

We watched her place a baby in the car seat and drive off.

"You let that bitch ride off with my child?" Nay screamed.

I opened the car and went to the trunk and grabbed my gloves.

"Why the fuck you still in the car? Bring your ass on," I threw a pair of gloves at her.

If this baby was Prince, we needed to make sure. I've killed a lot of bitches but this one was going to be different. Nay got out the car and followed me into the house. I had my own set of tools that I used for jobs like this. Nay picked up a picture of the girl and Kevin. We now knew why she was giving her a hard time.

"So he fucking this bitch? I don't really give a fuck about that. Let me see if the baby she got is my son," Nay said marching past me and down the hall.

It didn't take long before I heard shit crashing in the other room.

I got down the hall and Nay was holding her son's outfit he had on the night he got kidnapped. I knew it was his because I was the one who bought it and had his initials placed on the seat of the outfit.

"You know what we gotta do, right? Get your muthafuckin' feelings in check, bitch, because once we off this hoe, we got to get the hell up out of Dade County. This shit is only going to bring more damn heat once Kevin knows you got Prince back," I told Nay.

I'd been ignoring Dre all day and now I had to answer because he was Facetiming me and texting. I ignored the Facetime call and called him.

"Breya, I swear to God if you doing some shit you ain't got no business doing I'm not fucking with you no more," he barked in the phone.

"Calm your ass down. I'm doing something for Nay and it's private and personal. I'll call you back in a little bit. I love you," I rushed off the phone.

I looked at Nay pacing back and forth. She was obviously angry and she had every right to be. I wanted to make this shit worth our while.

"Let's fuck some shit up," I told Nay.

A smile crept across her face with confirmation.

Nay

I sat at this chick's dining room table cleaning my gun, waiting on her to come home with my son. I wasn't going to kill her right away; no, of course I wasn't. I was going to beat the dog shit out of her for talking shit yesterday. I put my gun back together and made sure it was loaded. I hated dragging Breya's pregnant ass in my shit. But she was my best friend, and she would've been mad if I did all this shit on my own. We went through all this bitch's shit. We fucked her house up by pouring Crisco grease over her furniture, poured out her nail polish on her clothes, broke all her shit up, cut up her mattress and bleached up her work uniforms.

I found out her name was Syriah and she was Kevin's little main chick. She was Stefano's niece and she was the one that was in my house. She was young so I see why Kevin picked her because she thought he was some god. She hadn't met God yet. I was about to be her worst enemy.

I peeped out the blinds as Breya stood on the other side of the door. She was finally pulling up after being gone for almost five hours. It only made me madder that I watched her get out the car and kiss my son in the mouth.

"Breathe, bitch! We can't have no mistakes with this hoe and she works at a federal prison," Breya whispered.

I bit the side of my jaw as she turned the key and entered the jet black house. She turned the small lamp on by the sofa.

"What the hell happened to my house?" she looked around. She placed my son down in his bouncer, yet she still hadn't noticed us.

"I'm not cuffed anymore, hoe. You still got some pressure you need to get off?" I emerged from where I was.

"Ronaysha?"

"Ohhhh, you know exactly who I am. Would that be because you stole my got damn son or because you fucking his daddy?" I slapped the shit out of her.

"You ain't shit, bitch. Kevin don't want your fat ass."

"Is that what he tells y'all hoes? Bring your ass here," I dragged her by her long brunette hair into the kitchen away from my son. I had my plastic laid out for the fun I was about to have with this hoe. Breya made sure Prince was strapped in his car seat so once I was done with her we could be on our way home.

Before I could get the bitch taped up, she wanted to put up a fight. I was being nice but once she scratched me in the face, I had to put it to her ass. I didn't need any of my DNA under this bitch's nails.

"You thought you could beat my ass, didn't you?" I asked, taping her to the chair as tight as I could. "So you thought it was okay to come into my house and take my son?"

She started shaking her head violently. The tears rolled down her eyes. The same tough girl I ran into at the prison was not the same girl that was staring back at me. I felt sorry for her and I really didn't give her a chance to explain herself, but I didn't care. My mother-in-law was murdered in the process. I laid her left hand on the table and took the big chopping knife and took her fingers off. Her screams were muffled.

Breya walked into the kitchen with an evil look in her eyes. I hadn't been this ruthless in a while but when you put my son in danger for a nigga, this is what happens.

"Let me get a piece," Breya begged.

Snatching the tape of her mouth, she pulled her tongue out her mouth and cut the tip of her tongue, causing blood to pour into her mouth. She took the tape and covered her mouth back up so the blood could fill up in her mouth. I was tired of playing already and was ready to get home with my son. I turned her gas stove on as I poured gasoline all over her.

"Get my son out of here and in the car," I told Breya.

Once she was gone and I heard the car start, I blew a kiss at her and walked out the kitchen. I pulled a lighter out of my pocket to light my blunt, taking a few pulls before I lit a piece of paper and placed it at the entrance of the kitchen. I watched a little while as the fire made its way up her body as I puffed my blunt. I was satisfied once the fire reached her torso. I could smell her flesh and all I could do was smile.

"Bye, little Ms. Syriah," I said, walking out the house.

***

I was finally back home with my son. I ran us a bath and relaxed in the water with him as he splashed. I wanted to breast feed him, but since he'd been gone, I had started back smoking and drinking and I didn't want to get that in his system; so I had to clean my system first. Now that he was home, I wasn't worried about shit. I wasn't going to let shit happen again. I washed his thick hair and washed him up. Persian called a meeting and I was taking my son with me. I didn't trust anybody with him at this point. It then hit me that I hadn't told Persian that I had my son back. He was going to beat my ass once I told him what I did.

I tried calling Tank but his phone was going straight to voicemail. I was already thinking he was up to no good with my trifling ass cousin Camellia, but knowing Tank, she wasn't his type. The other side of me was still like, he a man and a man ain't never turned no pussy down. Camellia threw pussy around like Santa throwing candy in a parade, with her nasty ass. My uncle Lou really didn't like her, but they tried to kill her in Cuba so he took her in. Now the only way to get rid of her was to kill her, and he'd been waiting on something to kill her for.

I got Prince and I dressed and got his bag ready. I jumped right back in my motherly role like he wasn't even gone. He was such a happy baby and I was glad she didn't harm my baby in any way. I would be able to rest more once I put a bullet in the middle of Kevin's head. He was a thorn in my flesh and I knew it was going to cause more problems since his bitch was dead, but I'll cross that bridge when I get there.

Persian

I squeezed on my stress ball as I waited on everyone to pile into the warehouse. Shit was getting hot and I was about to shut everything down. Some people were going to be mad but if they were smart, they should've been saving. I think it was time to let the young folks have this shit. I may have been thinking off of impulse, but I had a few businesses that I thrived off of and this shit was stressing me out knowing the Feds were watching us again. I couldn't chance anybody getting locked up and snitching.

Breya texted on her phone while we waited on Nay. I couldn't conduct the meeting without her since Tank was not here; she had to take his spot. I peeped Breya's phone and saw she was texting Nay.

"Tell her I said get her ass here now," I leaned over and told Breya.

"She outside and needs some help with Prince."

Breya covered her mouth once she let it slip out. I chewed on the side of my jaw because once again, my damn sister didn't listen. I heard her heels clicking against the floor. The cooing coming from my nephew eased my tension. I got up and snatched my nephew out of my sister's arms.

"You know damn well he don't need to be here. We never know what may pop off in this bitch. Oh, and don't think I'm not going to slap the shit out of you about being sneaky and shit. Sit your ugly ass down," I said between clenched teeth.

I placed kisses on my nephew's cheek as I looked at my team. This was probably going to be one of the hardest meetings we had. I loved each and every one of them, but I wouldn't feel right knowing I had the power to shut shit down and didn't. No one knew how much shit the Feds was pulling to take us down. I paid a lot of money to keep us all under the radar and because of it, I knew they had all of our pictures plastered over their bulletin boards with all of our trap houses.

"There's no better way to say this but to come out and say it. We got to shut this shit completely down, y'all. The Feds on our ass for real. I can't chance anything right now. I told you guys from the very beginning that in this game, you leave out either by jail or hell. We've made so much money together that I can't, as your leader, let that happen. When I said that, I was young. Now that I'm older and we rich now, let's think smart and get out."

"Persian, as long as I've been riding for you, this is the dumbest shit you ever said," one of the corner boys said.

Breya placed her gun on the table and I had my strap under the table, but I held on to my nephew. I hated Nay for bringing him here. Shit always popped off here.

"All I'm saying, big homie, is I lost a lot of shit to the streets and I been tired, but I couldn't come to you and say I wanted out. It's the dumbest, smartest shit you've said. I'll forever be a part of this family."

We all released our breath after he finished talking.

"I thought I was gon' have to off you in this bitch," I laughed. "Is everyone straight money wise? Now it's up to you if you want to keep selling, but your supplies will not come from me. You will have to find your own connect," I explained.

After we all came to an agreement, I ended the meeting. I let everyone know I was still a phone call away. I felt like a weight had been lifted off my shoulders. Breya and Dre were already working on shutting down the trap houses. Tank was handling business with Uncle Lou so everything was all good. It was just me, Nay, and my nephew left in the warehouse. She explained everything that happened and I was pissed. She tapped her nails on the marble table as I stared at her.

"You can talk now. You sitting there looking like Mama, but you know damn well I told you I was handling this shit, but you hardheaded as hell, Nay. You just put more fire under our ass and you getting messy as fuck. Don't get me wrong, I'm glad little man is back, but you had your ass three hours away and I didn't have eyes on you. Not to mention you went to jail for breaking that nigga's nose. I got to work to get that shit off your record. You really getting out of hand with your bullshit," I fussed.

"Are you done?" Nay asked.

I jacked her up by her shirt and got in her face.

"This shit about to ugly before it gets sweet. I just let go of over a million-dollars-a-month operation and you worried about am I finished. Nay, you might better get out my face before I hurt you. The muthfuckin' Feds on our ass! Do you want to go to jail, Ronaysha? Look at me! As your big brother, I'll never let that happen. You can't be out here murdering bitches and thinking shit sweet."

I released her once my nephew started stirring in my arms. I wiped the tears from her eyes and handed her Prince.

"Go home, Nay. I got to figure some shit out."

I pulled up at my house stressed the hell out. Neek stood at the door with a cute half-shirt on with her stomach popped out. I don't know why I loved her so much. We only had a few months before our baby was born. Neither of us wanted to know what we were having.

"How did it go?" she asked, grabbing my hand and leading me to the sofa.

"Shit still going wrong. Nay's hardheaded ass went and got Prince and caused more damage."

"Well, Persian, that is her son and she may have felt like y'all were moving too damn slow," Neek stated.

"I just move a little better than she does."

"You sure about that?" she raised her eyebrow.

"Not now, Neek," I pushed her off my lap.

She was still on that Deedra shit. I was over her sleeping with that bum ass nigga and she couldn't get over me getting my dick sucked. I hadn't slept with Neek since we tried this thing again. Every time I tried, all I could see is her opening her legs for another nigga.

"I have your dinner ready. I'm about to take Shanice to my mama's house and I'll be back."

I didn't respond, I just sat in the same spot putting some shit together in my head. Shanice came and placed a kiss on my jaw before running out the house. I loved the shit out of that little girl. Every decision I made was for my family. It was hard for me to let all that money go, but I guess it was time to get my grown man on and grind the smart way.

Tank

*N*ay was pissing me off not answering the phone. Camellia was standing in front of me half naked as she wound her body to rhythm of the beat that was coming through the speakers. Uncle Lou was throwing a party for me. I spent a whole week with him and now it was almost time for me to head home to my lady. All I could think about was getting in her guts. I talked to Nay one time since I'd been gone and I had a feeling she was up to no damn good. If she was, I would take it out on her pussy 'cause I wasn't going no damn where.

Camellia approached me, swaying her hips. She licked her lips and winked her eye at me. This little bitch was a certified freak. I don't know what type of marriage Uncle Lou was in, but this whole house was a damn freak show. I've had threesomes, shit, even foursomes, but since I had a taste of Nay's shit, a bitch couldn't even sniff my dick.

"My father will be occupied for the evening. Let me show you what my mouth do before you go home to my bitch ass cousin," she whispered in my ear, making sure to touch my ear with her lips.

She had my dick rising; hell, I was a man first. I was way in another country. Nay wouldn't find out anyway because Camellia wasn't allowed in the states. Who would it hurt? She knew I wasn't going to leave Nay, so why not have a little fun. I looked around and saw everyone was in their own world, so I slipped in my room with Camellia. I couldn't close the door fully before she started pulling at my jeans.

"I don't like that aggressive shit from a woman. Calm that down. You acting like a damn pit bull over the dick," I told her.

"I know it's big. I just want to see what I'm about to get into, that's all," she tried to kiss my lips.

"Bitch! I know since I been here your lips been on about twenty dicks and seven pussies. Don't ever in your life try to kiss me. Matter of fact, get your ass out. I don't know what the fuck I was thinking about," I yanked her by her arm and pushed her out the door, locking it behind her.

I almost fucked up. I gathered all my shit up and walked down to Uncle Lou's room. From the sound on the other side of the door, I knew what he was doing, but I didn't want to leave without him knowing, so I knocked anyway.

"Enter!" his voice boomed on the other side of the room.

I pushed the door open to see Uncle Lou tied up getting his dick rode by his wife while two other bitches pleasured each other next to them.

"I was just letting you know I'm heading out. I appreciate the hospitality."

"Camellia got you, didn't she? I'm going to kill her," he pushed his wife off of him.

"No! No! I'm just ready to get home, Uncle Lou, that's all," I explained.

"You're lying. I see her lipstick on your ear and on your cheeks."

"It's fine. Nothing happened."

"Nothing happened? You don't know my daughter very well. I will believe you this time. Just know Nay is more like my daughter than my niece. If I find out you lied to me we're going to have major damn issues. I will be in touch soon. Have a safe flight," he dismissed me.

I turned and ran right into Camellia. She had a look in her eyes that was strange. I moved past her and went to grab my things so I could head out. Uncle Lou had a car already waiting on me to head to the airport. I still had a few hours before my flight took off, so I got in the corner of the airport and took a nap. All I could think about was Nay's juicy ass and the wetness between her legs. I hoped I wasn't going home to no bullshit.

***

It felt good as fuck to be back on American soil. I powered on my phone to call Nay and to my surprise, she answered.

"Hello," she sung into the phone.

"Well got damn, you finally answered the fuckin' phone."

"Don't call me with no bullshit, Tank," she stated.

Hearing a baby in the background caught my attention.

"What is that in the background?"

"If you bring your ass home then you would know," she hung up.

Jumping on the shuttle so I could be taken to my car, I was more than ready to go home. I'd been eating so many black beans and rice in Colombia that I knew my stomach was ready to see my toilet. I jumped on the highway and headed home. The closer I got, the more I became anxious. I just prayed Nay kept her ass out of trouble. Since she had the baby, she was becoming more and more like her old self.

I could smell food before I even opened the door. The smell of lemon Pine-Sol hit my nose as well. Nay never surprised me with how she took care of home. For her to be a street chick, she knew how to take care of a man. Seeing her emerge from the kitchen with a long black lace teddy on made my dick hard. She had nothing on under it. She had just gotten waxed and her tattoos were looking sexy as fuck. I pulled my shirt off and scooped her ass up. We'd been beefing and barely sexing, but I was about to knock that shit out the park tonight.

"Fuck you doing with this on?" I asked before I ripped it.

"Damnit, Tank, that shit cost me a pretty penny," she whined.

"Do I look like I give fuck about what something cost? I'll buy twenty more of them little ass things. Bring me that pussy here."

I placed her against the stool and got on my knees. I spread her ass and listened for that nice pop her pussy did when it was wet. I connected my tongue with her clit before I covered it with my mouth to suck on it. She had no idea how much trouble she was in. Two weeks was too long to be away from her. I got her to the edge of her orgasm before I stopped and pulled my dick out. She gasped as I filled up her hole.

"Shitttt, this pussy tight."

The sound of her moans turned me on. I took it slow with her since she was running from the dick.

"Nay, don't start that running shit. Ain't no sense of having all this ass and wet pussy and can't take a big dick. I got to get your ass right. Stop running," I pressed into her back so she couldn't move.

Once I placed that arch in her back, I could feel my nut. The cries of a baby made my dick go limp and I slipped out of Nay.

"Is that my son?" I asked her, pulling my boxers up.

"He's hungry and that's why my breasts are leaking all over the floor. Let's finish this first," Nay pleaded.

"Hell no! My son home and you worried 'bout some dick. Your ass on punishment," I pinched her ass cheek.

I rushed down the hall to see my son lying in his bed. I went in the bathroom and brushed my teeth so I could place kisses all over him. I missed him so much. He was only missing for two weeks but he had gained so much weight. It made me feel good to know someone was at least taking care of him. Nay came in with an attitude but smiled once she laid eyes on me cuddling with Prince.

"You ready to explain how the fuck you got him back?" I eyed her.

I placed Prince down in his bed as Nay continued on with her story. Out of all she said, all I could hear her saying was she went to see that nigga. She was busy gloating on the fact that she killed the bitch that had our son that she didn't see me put him down. I was seeing red and the last thing I wanted to do was hit her. I wanted to jack her ass up but we would tear this small ass apartment up because Nay was going to fight back.

I grabbed a few items of clothes as she continued to talk. I told her ass not to have nothing to do with that nigga and again, she stepped all over my authority. A nigga was young but damn, I didn't like to be treated like a damn little ass boy. If she was my woman, I needed her to listen. I got my toothbrush and body wash and placed it in the bag.

"Where you going? You just got back?" Nay questioned.

"I thought I told you not to have any contact with that nigga?"

"I didn't. I mean, I did, but I found out where my son was though, Tank."

"So evidently, me and Persian wasn't doing it your way? It has to be Nay's way, huh? You don't listen to shit I have to say unless I'm eating your pussy or putting some dick up in you which you scared of any damn way. I'm not some little ass boy, Nay. All that controlling situations and shit you be doing is getting on my last nerve. You want to fuck with that nigga then do that. I don't know why I fell for your hardheaded ass anyway. Running up in you raw and shit and you driving three hours to see another nigga. Just because I didn't tell you my plan; I had a plan, Nay. Sometimes sitting your ass down and waiting would help. I'll come get Prince tomorrow, stay the fuck out my way when you see me."

I could see the hurt and anger in her face but I didn't give a fuck. Persian and I had plans to go to Miami and come back with Prince. We knew that's where he was but we couldn't tell Nay that for obvious reasons, with her hotheaded ass. Now she's killed a CO from a Federal prison. She fell right back into Kevin's trap. I walked out the apartment without looking back.

Nay

"Fuck niggas," I said out loud.

I was getting my son dressed so I could take him to work with me. I hadn't slept since Tank walked his childish ass out the door yesterday. I don't know what I did so bad besides bringing my son back home safe. Persian and Tank made it out to be something negative. I wasn't about to sit around this damn house and pout about a nigga. I've been there and done that shit with Kevin. If something so small pissed Tank off, then we had no business being together. If you ask me, he planned to come home and fuck the shit out of me and leave.

I placed some pillows around Prince as he slept on my bed. I went to get the scent of Tank off of me. I really needed to get out and start living a little bit, but being a mother was far more important to me. I wasn't letting another nigga come in and fuck my heart up and leave. That shit was far too easy for him. He was probably somewhere laid up with another female as I washed his semen from between my legs. Thank God I was on the pill; I couldn't take the chance of being pregnant again from a nothing ass nigga.

I grabbed my towel and entered the room. Seeing Tank sitting on the side of the bed made my heart flutter.

"I came to get Prince for the day. I called your phone but you didn't answer and I thought something was wrong," he said without looking at me.

"His bag is packed. I was going to take him to work with me. Remember to run his breast milk under some warm water to thaw it out," I reminded him.

"I've seen you do that shit a million times. I don't need you to tell me how to take care of my son. Have a good day at work," he sternly said.

He grabbed Prince and placed a kiss on his jaw. He threw the bag over his shoulder and walked out my room. I tried as hard as I could not to cry but I couldn't hold it in any longer. I walked into the closet and snatched my clothes off the hangers and grabbed a pair of heels off the shelf. I got dressed in a hurry so I could get out of this apartment. The smell of his cologne was still lingering well after he was gone.

I locked up the apartment and made sure I had my .40 in my purse. I never left the house without some type of heat on me. I took the drive to my restaurant first. I wanted to shut it down because it only brought bad memories, but Breya talked me out of it. I didn't spend much time here like I should. I paid my general manager well to handle all situations so I wouldn't have to. When I pulled up, I was happy to see the parking lot full. My chest tightened once I got out the car and made my way to the doors. This happened every time I was here. I briskly walked back to my car and locked the door. I called inside the restaurant and asked did they need me. Once everyone told me they were okay, I headed to my shoe store.

"Hey, Nay, I wasn't expecting you today. I'm glad you're here. For the past two days, you've been getting a lot of black roses delivered. I know what you've been going through so I've been throwing them out.

You just had some delivered."

I eyed her. I was glad I hired her because she picked up on my spirit, and she knew me better than I knew myself sometimes. I looked at the dozens of black roses sitting on the counter. I picked them up and took them into my office. I looked at the note attached and pulled it out. My hands went straight for my purse. Kevin was fucking with my mind.

"Ronaysha Maxwell, you're under arrest for distribution of narcotics." a Federal agent placed the cuffs on me, while the other one showed me the warrant.

"Please don't cuff me in my business. Can we do this outside? I'll freely go with you guys, just don't do this in my place of business," I begged.

The male federal officer shook his head yes. I breathed a sigh of relief. I had customers out on the floor and this was the last thing I needed. I called one of my managers in the office and gave her instructions on what I needed her to do before I was whisked out the door and placed in the back of an undercover truck.

"Damn, Kevin told me how fine you were but I wasn't expecting you to look this good," the male fed said. I looked him over and he was fine as hell.

"Why didn't I know he had something to do with this?" I rolled my eyes and looked out the window.

"I got to say he's a real live pussy nigga to give you up to lower his sentence. By the way, my name is Mulik," he said, holding his hand out for me to shake it.

"I don't really like talking to the pigs. You too damn fine to be working for these damn people."

He laughed, showing her perfect white teeth and deep dimple on the left cheek. He was dark with bushy eyebrows. His eyes were jet black, his baldhead and goatee made him look like he was in his thirties, but I wasn't sure.

"I don't like to be called a pig. More like the nigga that's going to get you out this shit if you agree to at least let me take you out?" he licked his lips.

I turned my head back to the window and closed my eyes tightly. The vision of Tank and my son popped up. Why was I thinking about Tank, he left me? He dumped me without a good reason.

"I'll give you some time to think about it. We're here anyway. I'll be in the interrogation room to talk to you in a little bit," he winked.

The cuffs were finally placed on me as I was walked into the precinct. The nerve of Kevin to rat me out so he could get out. I was clean of any distribution charges. I hadn't touched drugs in years. The only time you would catch me on the streets was if some shit was popping off. Persian made sure I was never seen on the scene. Only thing they could have on a bitch right now is the murder of Syriah. Hopefully, Mulik didn't come in here with the bullshit because I didn't have shit to say. The door popped open and his fine ass walked in. My eyes took in his body; he had a muscular build under his suit. He had great taste because his cologne and the fabric of his clothes told on him. My eyes went down to his third leg. It was massive, so massive that even his briefs couldn't hold it.

He placed what I assumed was my file down on the table and sat down across from me and opened it. For it to be a file against me, it was pretty thick. My throat became dry because maybe they did have some shit against me. Whatever they had I wasn't saying shit. He pulled out some pictures of me and Tank, some of just me shopping, my son, and me and Breya. None of them were incriminating so I was able to breath.

"I'm shocked that a woman of your caliber has a clean record. You've kept your nose clean for a long time. I can't stand to see girls like you come in here because of a hateful, bitter boyfriend. I've been following you for some time now and the only thing I could notice was you went missing to Miami a few days," he eyed me.

I swallowed hard. This was it for me. I kept my eyes trained on him; I wasn't about to show any signs of fear.

"I think that was around the time you went to see him and broke his nose. Not soon after, I get a call that he wanted to talk to me. I thought it was funny that you broke his nose and then he wanted to tell like a little kid."

"So am I under arrest or did you just bust up in my damn business causing a scene to tell me that Kevin's a little bitch? I already know that."

"So what's up with you and him?" Mulik slid the picture of Tank passionately kissing me outside of our house right after I had my son.

The tears were stinging my eyes because right now, I wanted Tank so bad. I wanted him to grab me just like that, squeeze my ass and kiss me hard. I loved him. Maybe I fell for him too fast but any nigga eating pussy like he does would make anyone fall in love.

"He's my boyfriend," I lied. I really didn't lie; he broke up with me but I didn't break up with him. His dick belonged to me and if I found out he was giving it up, him and the bitch I caught him with were going to be dead.

"So you're taken?" Mulik raised his eyebrow.

"Yes I am," I replied.

"That's interesting," he rubbed his goatee. "Well, I guess I have my work cut out for me."

"Am I free to get out this bitch or what? I need to call a ride."

"Well, I could hold you here for this small warrant I found for an unpaid ticket," he slipped a ticket from the other side of the folder.

This fine muthafucka was slick and I had to watch his ass. How he go from telling me my record was clean and then come with a damn warrant for a damn ticket when he find out I got a nigga.

"I'll sit in this bitch for a day about that pussy ass ticket," I bluntly told him.

"That mouth," he laughed. "Since you a bad ass, I'll book you for this ticket. Don't say I didn't try to help you. I'll see your fine ass around. Hopefully not with that lil' young ass nigga," he got up and walked out. Thirty minutes later, I was booked and sitting in a holding cell.

***

"Maxwell, you made bail!" I heard them yell and the door popped open.

How the hell I made bail so fast was beyond me, but I wasn't about to argue about it. It was nasty as hell in here and smelled like a drunk person had pissed on the floor. I got everything I came in here with and walked through the metal detector to see Tank.

"I'll see you around, Ronaysha," Mulik smiled.

Tank's expression showed murder. I grabbed my son from his arms and walked out the door. My life was some bullshit right now and my son was the only balance I had. Once we made it to the house in silence, I knew once I came out the shower, Tank was going to start with the shit.

Tank

I rocked Prince to sleep while Nay took a shower. I wasn't even going to bother her about going to jail. She was solid and I wasn't worried about her running her mouth. She had just as many bodies as me, if not more. What I was about to question her about was that pussy nigga smiling and licking his lips at her like he could taste her pussy on his lips. Once Prince was good and asleep, I placed him in his bed and cut his monitor on so I could hear him. I entered the bedroom I used to share with Nay as she laid in the bed with her tablet and laptops. I knew she was giving out the last payments to the workers but that shit could wait.

"Who the fuck was that police ass nigga grinning and shit in your face?" I mugged her.

Seeing her laugh pissed me off. I didn't find shit funny and if she didn't answer me soon, I was gon' tear this damn apartment up. I had a lot of anger built up because I couldn't take off Kevin's head, and she 'round this bitch letting a nigga smile in her face.

"Tank, we not together, right?" she looked up from her devices for assurance.

Shit, she was right. I was really just fucking with her with this breaking up shit. I guess she wasn't with the little boy games.

"That ain't what I asked you, Nay."

"I know what you asked me, but I'm not answering you because we're not together, you feel me," she continued what she was doing.

"Let me find out you fucking that police ass nigga, I'll make sure to bury both of y'all muthafuckas together. Now try me, Nay," I threatened.

"Tank, with the shit I been through, the last thing your little ass want to do is throw damn threats. I may just think you serious and kill you first, now try me."

I snatched her by her legs and yanked her to the edge of the bed. We both had some tension that we needed to release. She was fucking my heading up big time and I know I was doing the same thing to her. I don't care what happened between us, I wasn't about to let another nigga come and take what belonged to me. Everything about Nay belonged to me and I would kill any nigga that thought he was going to sniff round her shit.

I ripped her damn boy shorts off, leaving a red mark on her skin. She didn't even try to fight against me; she freely opened her legs. My dick was already hard as I entered her wetness. Nay flipped me over like a little bitch and took control. That only rocked me up harder. She usually only rode my dick when she felt like I was slaying her ass and she couldn't control me.

"Ride that dick, Nay," I slapped her ass. Spreading her cheeks, I rammed my dick in her to meet her thrust. She creamed all over my dick.

"Look at that shit. You don't want that uppity nigga, do you? You want a young thug to milk this pussy, don't you?" I eyed her.

"Yessss, daddy," she moaned, throwing her head back. I gripped her titties and enjoyed the ride before I was about to flip her ass back over.

"Bring me that pussy," I flipped her over, dragging her back to the edge of the bed. I spread her legs like a peace sign and slow stroked her until we both came.

***

Slipping my arm from under Nay, I eased out of the bed and put my clothes back on. I knew I was messing up by sleeping with her but I was confused as hell. I wanted her but I was mad at her and wanted to punish her. The other part of me didn't want nobody else to have her either, so I felt like if I kept her dicked down then she wouldn't have the time to entertain another man. I grabbed my cell phone and walked down the hall to check on Prince before I walked out the door. I was staying in my mama's old house. I don't know why I didn't just sell the house. She loved this house, so I decided to just crash here, right in the middle of my hood. It was going on about three in the morning and a nigga was tired from sexing Nay. I took a quick shower and climbed in my mama's bed. I could still smell her Bath and Body Works in the sheets, no matter how many times I changed them. It didn't take long for me to close my eyes and dream of my mama.

Banging on my door woke me up out of my dream. I missed my mama like hell and whoever was at the door was 'bout to get cussed out because I was just chilling and tripping off old times with my mama. Unaware that I only had on a pair of boxers, I answered the door.

"You got a bitch in here, Tank?" Nay pushed me out the way.

"What damn time is it? Where the hell Prince at?"

Nay marched around the house looking for anything out of place. Once she couldn't find anything, she stood by the door with wet eyes. A nigga felt bad for leaving her like that, but I couldn't really express the feelings I was feeling. I mean, I know it was love, but sometimes it felt deeper than that.

"Tank, I'm trying to stay as calm as I can. If you not going to fuck with me, please leave me the hell alone. That goes for sex, conversation, and my son. We are no longer tied together for business so what we had is over. I can't keep giving you all of me and you running like a little ass boy," she expressed with tears falling down her pretty face.

"Wait now. Prince is my damn son. I signed my name on his birth certificate so all that other bullshit you saying is irrelevant. Was a nigga wrong for fucking your guts up and leaving? Hell yea, and it won't happen again," I explained.

"You right it won't happen again, because I won't be opening my legs up to you ever again," she said before walking off.

"It don't matter what your ugly ass say, you'll forever be Tank's girl with your fat ass," I yelled at her.

She shot me a bird and pulled off. I was messing up big time and I needed to get my emotions in check if I was going to mess with a female of Nay's caliber.

Persian

I laid in my bed smoking, catching up on any and everything I could watch. I hadn't been in the house this much in years. With me and Neek on bad terms I mainly stayed in my room to keep the tension down between us. I didn't talk to her, but I made sure she had what she needed; but I couldn't stomach the sight of her sometimes. I still had some reservations about the baby she was carrying. I mean, in my head she could've been pregnant by me, but I don't know how long she was messing with old dude. The shit was a mystery to me and I still felt like her ass be lying 'bout shit. Only time will tell. She was about to graduate college so I bought her a nice lil' truck. She was going to need something to drive the children in. Shanice just started dancing for a local studio so that was keeping her from the house some; and I was happy to have some peace.

I checked my phone periodically because I was so used to it ringing or notifying me about a text. I did have a text from some chick I met at one of my groundbreaking events. Building housing in the hood was my new venture and all the hood chicks be at every event trying to get housing. She was nice looking but she wasn't what I wanted. I still don't know how she got my number, but she was needy as hell and she was about to go to the block list. I never liked a woman that still texted a man that constantly left her on read. I have yet to respond to her, but she still sends nudes, and texts to my phone. I deleted the text and placed the phone down when Shanice ran in the room and jumped in the bed.

"Daddy, look at our new outfits we wearing to the parade," Shanice said.

I opened the little piece of fabric. There was no way in hell I was letting my little seven-year-old wear this.

"Shanice, where your mama at? Go get her and you go in your room for a minute," I told her.

"Daddy, please don't fuss at mama about the outfit. The dance instructor said we'll have tights on."

"Shanice, go get your mama," I sternly said.

That's what was wrong with a lot of these young girls that hung on the block. They were still in school but were fucking out both sides of their pants leg. Shanice was not going to be one of them. I already had her college fund put up for whatever college she decided to go to.

"You wanted me?" Neek came in huffing and puffing. She hardly came in my room. I gave her our old room and I slept in the guest room. Did I ever want to sleep with her? Yes, I did. I missed everything about her, but I hated when I couldn't trust somebody.

"What the hell going on with that outfit?" I sat up in the bed. I forgot I didn't have any clothes on so my dick slipped out the slit of my boxers. Seeing Neek lick her lips made me rock up, but I wasn't going there with her. She wouldn't taste this shit until I knew the paternity of the kid she was carrying. I slipped my dick back in my boxers and threw some covers over myself. She rolled her eyes and laughed.

"She will be covered up. The only skin you will see is a little bit of her stomach," Neek explained.

My phone got my attention so I grabbed it. I shook my head and smiled looking at the picture. I swear this girl never quits. I was so busy looking at her dildo with her cream on it that I didn't see Neek walking towards me until my phone was snatched out my hand. I didn't even try to get it back from her. It wasn't like I ever slept with the girl. Maybe Neek needed to see she had a little competition. I grabbed the remote and flipped the TV.

"I swear I can't stand you!" Neek threw my phone at me, hitting me in the head.

"Man, you better stop that shit now."

"So is this why you can't touch me; because you 'round here sleeping with a female that can fit a truck up her pussy? I swear you nasty as hell. Why you still holding me and my daughter here again? Oh, yea that's right. You don't want nobody else to have me. Not only that but you got man issues. I fucked up just like you did and you can't get over the fact somebody else had me," she taunted.

"If you don't want to end up dead just like him, I advise your black ass to get the hell out of my room," I grunted.

"No, you gon' hear what I got to say. You always want to dictate when we talk. I'm sick of the shit to be honest. Since you want to jack your dick to a picture then do you. Don't try to sneak touch me or nothing. All we need to worry about is co-parenting these kids. I hate I'm about to have a baby by you," she said walking away.

I yanked her ass by her shirt without getting off the bed. I glared in her eyes as tears ran down the side of her face. I could see all the hurt running down her face as each tear was released. I was still hurting too. Yea, what she said was the truth. What man wanted his lady sleeping with another man? You find me one and I'll put a bullet in his head. I still wanted Neek badly but my heart was messed up. Since we'd been going through this I hadn't even entertained another female. I beat my meat in the shower plenty of nights just thinking about her.

"We got to get this shit right, Neek. I'm tired, man. I'm not on the streets anymore. I'm in the house most of the time unless I'm out handling legal business. All this not speaking to each other is childish and I'm sick of it. I got some growing up to do and so do you. Stop that crying, bae," I wiped her tears. "I really do love you. A part of me wants to hate you but I can't; and as long as Shanice is between us and this child, then we're connected for life."

I bent down and kissed her lips passionately. The fire was still there between us. I knew she was my rider, we just both had some work to do. I was going to start by changing my number so I couldn't get any more nudes. I kissed her neck and her scent that I missed so much filled my nose. I could tell by her body language she missed me too, but I couldn't give it to her right now. I may hurt the baby.

"Can a nigga get a meal?"

"I was about to cook before you called me all the way up these stairs," she laughed.

I moved so I could help her sit up. I brushed her hair down with my fingers. I didn't need Shanice asking what we were doing because she was super nosey.

"I'll call you when the food is ready. I need you to finish what you started later," she pleaded with her eyes.

"I don't want to hurt the baby though," I told her.

"Persian, you will not hurt the baby," she laughed before walking out.

Breya

*D*re and the kids had an appetite. I was the one pregnant, but Dre was eating like he was the one pregnant. I was at Publix getting groceries for the week. My baby had just started moving in my stomach so I was rushing, trying to get home so Dre could feel the little flutters. I turned the corner and ran right into Blake's buggy.

"Bitch, you better watch where you going," she winked at me.

I think she forgot about the ass whooping I gave her outside the club that night. I tried to get around her before I turned aisle seven into a murder scene. Blake blocked the aisle so I couldn't get around her.

"Look, I'm being nice right now. I really don't want to be but since I'm raising your kids, I do want to make it back to them without a scratch. I would hate to go home and tell them I had to beat the hell out of their mama at the grocery store. Now you can move or get your ass beat in front of your little friend here."

"You won't catch me slipping anymore. I don't have nothing to lose," she came from around the buggy and swung at me. Instead of her fist connecting to me, it was a blade that cut me above my eye. The blood instantly started pouring from my cut. I had to think fast because she was coming back towards me, swinging the blade like a wild child. I didn't have time to pull my gun out, so I was going to have to square up with her, and I did just that. She was taller than me, but I knew all the pressure points to break her ass down to my size. She swung again and missed, causing her body to turn slightly, and I took that as my opportunity to grab her. When I grabbed her, she came back with the blade, slicing me across my chest and down to my stomach. I could feel the burn coming from the cut but I couldn't stop now. People were crowding around us and I could see her friend out of the corner of my eye trying to sneak me. I picked up a jar of spaghetti sauce and threw it at her.

"Bitch, don't come near me or I'll break her damn neck," I threatened.

"Ma'am, calm down. You're bleeding," a stocker said to me.

I had my knees on both of Blake's arms. I couldn't chance her cutting me again. My shirt was cut open and it was dark red blood all over the floor. She was screaming she couldn't breathe and I really didn't give a fuck. If she was strong enough, she could've easily lifted up my 130-pound frame, but once I felt the blade run across my stomach, I turned into a monster. This bitch was trying to kill my baby.

My body was snatched up off of her and we were both placed in cuffs.

"Sir, she needs medical attention. She wasn't the one that started the altercation; it was little red bone right there," a witness stated.

I remained in cuffs but was placed on a stretcher and sent to the hospital. All I could think about was catching her ass somewhere and slitting her throat. If I wasn't in a public place, I would've killed her and her friend and left them stankin' in an alley, dumb bitch. My adrenaline was rushing something bad, to the point that I didn't feel any pain. My blood pressure was high and the EMT told me several times to calm down. How was I supposed to calm down when a normal day of grocery shopping turned into an altercation with a bitch I used to fuck?

Several stitches in my face, chest and stomach; I was barely holding on to the baby. Dre sat in the corner shaking his leg and staring off into space. In the midst of us fighting, I took a pretty hard fall on my stomach. The fall was so hard that my baby was traumatized by it. I'd been bleeding ever since I got to the hospital and they were just waiting on me to bleed my child out.

I wanted to get out of the bed and comfort Dre because his shaking leg stopped and it was replaced with tears as the heartbeat of our child became more faint. I felt like it was all my fault. I should've tried harder to leave the situation, but backing down was hard for me. It may have been the short people syndrome my mama always told me I had. My cramping started getting worse and I figured this was it. I didn't think I would ever have kids so I enjoyed the moments I had with my child. If Dre was up to it, we could try again. I had a feeling he was going to hate me after this. I turned my head away from him and let my tears fall as my child escaped me. They already informed me that I would still practically give birth because I was a little over four months pregnant.

"I'll be back," Dre stated, getting up out the dark corner.

"Where you going?"

"I'm about to go handle some shit right quick and I promise I'll be back, Breya."

"Dre, please don't leave me like this," I cried.

He closed the door and walked over to my bed. He climbed his big frame in the bed and cuddled up behind me. He placed his nose in my neck and waited for the doctors to come in and perform the procedure. This was going to be hard on both of us, but our bond was strong.

Nay

After checking on Breya, I decided to head to the mall and grab a few things. Prince was getting big and he needed some clothes as well. I was starting to feel a little better since I completely let Tank go. I still thought about him, but it was time for me to get myself together and stop letting men run my mind and body. The Mall at Millenia was my favorite spot to shop because it had all my stores I liked to shop in. My first stop was going to be Versace to grab a pair of shoes I saw online. After getting a few things, Prince was now sleep and my feet were hurting in my pumps. I had his stroller packed down with bags and I had both hands filled with bags as well. The struggle was real, and today was the day I didn't use valet. I wasn't expecting to spend so much time here, but I saw so much stuff that I couldn't help myself.

"Let me help you with that."

I turned around to see who would be so nice to help. My throat got real dry once I saw that it was Mulik. I turned on my heels and walked away as fast I could.

"Hey, wait! I'm trying to help, nothing more," he explained.

I slowed my pace down because I did need the help and my feet were aching. I finally stopped so he could grab all the bags out my hands.

"Take your shoes off. I'll carry those too. I know you got a pair of them expensive ass flats in that Tory Burch bag you carrying."

He was absolutely right. I always carried flats with me, but I didn't want to stop and change so I was going to force my way to the car. He held his muscular arm out so I could have something to balance on as I took my shoes off. His cologne was breathtaking. I knew my perfumes and colognes, and this cologne he wore was very expensive. I knew he couldn't afford it on his salary.

"Are you wearing Clive Christian cologne?" I looked at him.

"Yes I am. Do you like it?"

"It's nice or whatever. I'm just a fan of fragrances, that's all."

We got to my Jag and I popped the trunk. Prince was still sleep and I was glad because I had just started back breastfeeding him. I knew once he woke up he was going to be ready, but I wanted to at least make it home and get comfortable first.

"So, this is my second time running into you. This time I'm not arresting you though," he nervously laughed.

"Do I make you nervous or something?"

"I don't know, why you ask?" he looked at me.

"You do this nervous little chuckle. It's cute, if you are nervous," I smiled at him.

"Well, as beautiful as you are, any man should be nervous. I was wondering could I offer you my number so I could take you out," he chuckled again.

I had a bunch of thoughts running through my head right now. Mulik was the feds and I had a lot of shit that I'd done. That shit with Kevin's girlfriend was still running across the news, making me nervous, but they didn't have any leads because she was so badly burned. I could hear Persian's voice fussing about fucking with the police, and then there was Tank. I did just get out of a relationship with him but I missed his ass something serious. I didn't want to be seen with Mulik and ruin my chances with Tank forever.

"Let me hold your phone," I told him.

I put my number in his phone and finished strapping Prince in.

"I'll give you a call," he stated before walking backwards so he could check me out.

I got in the car and hit reverse when my car started beeping. I looked in the camera to see Tank's Maserati blocking me in. He got out without a shirt on and a pair of joggers. I bit my bottom lip as he approached my car. I made sure my doors were locked and windows up. I could tell by how he was walking he was with the shits.

"Open this damn door," he hit the window.

"Get your ass away from my car, Tank," I said through the tinted window.

"I told you about fucking with me, didn't I? You 'round this bitch giving out your number and shit? Just know when they find his ass missing it's your fault. Take your ass home and I'll meet you there," he got back in his car and pulled off. Where the hell was mall security when I needed them? Tank had me thinking we were still together by the way he was acting. I didn't feel like going home but where else was I going to go? I wasn't about to bother Breya with my damn problems when she had just lost her baby.

Just like he said, Tank was there sitting in his car waiting. Prince was up and already crying. When I got him out of the seat, he was already going for my breast, so all my shit I had in the car could wait. I sat on the sofa and fed Prince while Tank sat across from me, mugging me.

"Why the hell you here?" I finally asked him.

"Why the hell you got your number changed?"

"It was time for a change," I shrugged.

He rubbed his head and shook his head like he was thinking about something. He wasn't going to show out while I had Prince in earshot. He hardly ever raised his voice around him. Once Prince was done eating, Tank grabbed him and burped him. While he spent time with him, I got all of my stuff out of the car. I was praying Tank got Prince tired and ready for bed before he left.

"Your boyfriend just called your phone," Tank smiled. "Don't worry, I told him you made it home safe to zaddy."

"Stay off my stuff, Tank. I'm not playing with your childish ass. Don't hate on the next man because he got manners."

"Manners? That nigga the police. He just keeping tabs, and you so dumb you don't see it, but I won't bother shit else of yours. Go on your little dates and stuff with his old ass. The first time I think you giving that pussy up, he's dead. Get your ass out the way so I can spend some time with my son. Think you just gon' date and go on with your life easily, got another thing coming," he mumbled as he walked up the hall to Prince's room.

He sounded so dumb. I didn't care though. I didn't agree to go on a date I just gave him my number. I did want a mature conversation since Tank was always acting rude. It felt good to make a man nervous. I sat on my bed and thought about that date after all. Maybe Tank could watch Prince while I stepped out. I was pushing it a little bit but when the time came, I would build up the nerve to ask him. Until that time, we would work on the co-parenting thing first.

Neek

$\mathcal{P}$ersian and I were starting to get back on track. It was still hard for me to get him to fully trust me. I knew it was going to be hard work but now it was beginning to be too much. The biggest thing I wanted to do was pay him his money back. Since I got some of the best skills at Full Sail, I started doing book covers for the urban books and doing photography on the side to get the money back. I got Persian to agree to do a paternity test before the child was born so that could ease some of the tension in our house. Today was the day we got the results. I was confident as I walked to the mailbox.

I fumbled through the mail as I walked back to the house. The letter I was looking for was at the bottom of the stack. I stopped on the steps to rip it open. My hands started shaking and the tears started stinging my eyes. I walked in the house and took one look around. Shanice was at dance practice and it was Persian's turn to pick her up after his meeting, so I had time to do what I needed to do. I placed all of the mail on the table expect the paternity test. I made sure to place that on Persian's bed.

I walked in my room and packed all my shit. When I say all, I mean everything. Persian had just bought me a new truck and it took me weeks to drive because I didn't feel worthy of driving it. It took me several trips and a few breaks to catch my breath, but I got it all in. I looked at Shanice's room and wiped the tears. I closed the door and locked the house before climbing in my truck and pulling off. I had no idea what I was doing but I needed to get away. I drove to the gas station and gassed up before getting on 95 North with no destination in mind. I hadn't even told my mama.

I made it to the Georgia line before I stopped and grabbed something to eat. I looked at my watch and knew within the next fifteen minutes, I was going to get a call from Persian. I sat in the car and ate before I started back driving north. I just wanted to be somewhere secluded where no one knew me. Just like clockwork, Persian called me. I hit the answer button on my steering wheel.

"Hello," I said nervously.

"Where the fuck you at?" his voice boomed through the speakers.

"I'm leaving, Persian. I'm already gone and I don't wan—"

"So you leave my muthafuckin' money and the results to a paternity test laying on the bed, and leave like a little bitch instead of facing me?" he cut me off.

"Don't call me a bitch, Persian."

"I'm not calling you a bitch, Neek, I said you running like one. Get your ass back home with my child, Neek, or I swear when I find you I'll kill you and take my child. Why the hell you running? What am I supposed to tell Shanice?" his voice cracked.

I was being selfish and I knew it.

"Neek, do you hear me talking to your ass? You know what—fuck it. Take your ass on. It ain't like you got shit. I'll take care of Shanice, don't even fucking worry about her. You better make sure you take good damn care of my child, Neek. Don't come crawling your ass back because it's gon' be too late. It's my fault I fucked with your young ass. I'm a grown ass man so I'll make sure I tell Shanice her mama loved her but she was too damn dumb to stay and fight for what she loved," he said before hanging up in my face.

I couldn't drive any further. My heart was just ripped out of my chest. I was so used to Persian chasing me but I really took it too far this time. Finding out I was carrying Persian's baby was what I wanted, but I needed a minute to breathe and Persian wasn't going to willingly let me breathe. I pulled over outside of South Carolina and got a room. I balled up in the bed and cried myself to sleep.

Nay

"Breya, please tell me why you already out and about instead of resting," I looked at Breya's scars. She was going to have a permanent scar running across her face. Blake better be glad I wasn't with Breya that day because I would've murdered her on sight and sat my ass in a jail cell. Blake got her ass beat time she got behind the walls in Orange County. Breya had cousins doing time and they got word about what happened. Let's just say they had to ship Blake's ass off to Georgia to keep her ass alive.

"I'm fine. You know me better than anyone. I'm not about to stay my ass in the house. Now tell me about this damn man that got your fast ass on the way to the mall to buy clothes."

"His name is Mulik. I met him when he came and pulled me out of my damn business on some drug charges. I still believe it was staged but I can't prove it. I ran into him again at the mall a few weeks ago and he helped me get my stuff in the car."

"So wait a damn minute. He the police?" Breya quizzed.

"Umm, yea," I bit my nail.

"Bitch! You know we don't fuck with the pigs."

"But we all legal now. What's the big deal?" I asked.

"The big deal is that we still murkin' bitches 'round here. We legal but we both know at the drop of a dime we can be drawn back into the streets if that's what Uncle Lou says to do."

Breya had me thinking. Nobody would just let me live. I continued to drive to the mall. Breya and I shopped and enjoyed lunch until it was time for me to drop her off and get ready for my date.

"Damn, he getting on my nerves," I got out the car to see Tank carrying Prince up to the front door. I had the locks changed so he couldn't come and go as he wanted.

"I got to drop Prince off because some shit came up."

"You lying but it's cool. Give me my baby," I took Prince out his arms.

"I ain't got to lie to you. You ain't my girl, shit."

I don't know why that hurt my feelings once he released that from his lips. I grabbed the baby bag from him and went into the house, slamming the door in his face. That's what I get for falling in love with a young ass little boy. I placed Prince in his playpen as I dug in my purse for my phone to call Mulik.

"Hey, beautiful," he said, making me smile.

"Hey. I hate to call you at the last minute and cancel but my babysitter fell through," I explained.

"Baby daddy acting an ass, huh? It's all good. Bring him with you. If I'm going to date his mama I might as well see if he at least likes me."

"Are you sure?"

"Yea, and make sure you wear some damn tennis shoes. Leave them expensive heels in the closet for another day," he said before we hung up.

I picked me and my son out some fresh clothes. I cleaned him up and changed him before I got myself dressed. I knew Mulik knew my address but I told him I would meet him. I didn't want to chance Tank's crazy self popping up on us.

"You look good with your tennis shoes on. Let me guess, them Fashion Nova jeans? I'm sure they are the only jeans that can hold all that ass."

"Please," I batted my lashes.

"I promise to be good," he threw his hands up.

We walked into the theme park. It wasn't as packed as I thought it would be. I couldn't wait until my son was old enough to enjoy Fun Spot. Mulik was the perfect gentleman. Prince ended up leaving the park with several big bears. Mulik told me he went to college on a basketball scholarship. His father made him get into law enforcement but he hated it. He told me he was divorced with no kids and was trying to open up a barber shop so he could leave the feds. I was impressed with his conversation as we ate dinner. Mulik was showing me a different side. I was from the hood and he was from the suburbs but he had a thing for hood chicks.

"I really enjoyed you guys tonight," he pulled me in and placed a kiss on my neck.

It was sexy or whatever, but my body didn't react the way it did when Tank pulled me in.

"I enjoyed myself too."

"Can I kiss you? It's okay if you say no, I totally understand what no means," he chuckled.

"I can't," I confessed.

He released me and played in Prince's curls as he sat in his stroller chewing on a teething ring. I didn't know what else to say to him. I was looking forward to spending more time with him though.

"I guess this is see you next time?" he eyed me.

"Yea, next time."

I was finally able to breathe once I was in my car and on the way home. I had to get some gas before I headed in the house for the night. I was going to spend time with Persian and Shanice tomorrow, and I didn't want to stop in the morning.

A Maserati pulled up to the pump next to me. I wasn't in the mood for Tank to be following me and shit, so I ignored him while I pumped my gas. When the door opened, the weed smoke escaped the car and instead of him getting out, it was a bitch.

"I know damn well…"

She knew who I was because she eyed me and laughed as she walked in to pay for her gas. Dumb ass didn't even have a debit card because clearly she was walking in to pay for her gas with cash. He could've gassed up for her, with her stuntin' ass. The passenger door opened and Tank hopped out with a blunt burning his damn jeans. I didn't have time for this shit. I had my son with me so I politely got my ass back in my Jag and attempted to pull off, but Tank jumped in front of my car. He was obviously drunk and high because his eyes were red and low. I eased my foot off the brake so Tank would see that I would run his ass over.

"You gon' run your nigga over?" he smiled, revealing a gold grill.

"Childish ass," I said out loud.

"Tank, come on, baby," the girl whined. I guess he had a thing for whiners. She had a bad ass frontal on but the color made my stomach hurt. Who the hell wore pink hair? She was a baddie so he did well. I wasn't a hater.

"Tank, move your ass out the way. Your girlfriend calling you anyway," I said with my head out the window.

"I'll be by later," he said with assurance. "You know that's daddy's pussy," he laughed.

"Get your drunk ass out the way," I tapped his leg with my car so he could leave.

He finally moved and hit the trunk of my car as I pulled off. I guess since we were moving on I could take it there with Mulik. Call me what you want but Tank wanted to play games, let's play. I was the queen of games.

I got home and put Prince to bed. About one in the morning, Tank came beating at the door. He called my phone several times until I finally cut it off. This is what he wanted. He was a reincarnation of Kevin and I wasn't about to go through the off and on relationship thing again.

"Nay, open the door before I shoot the knob off this door!" Tank yelled.

I cut my phone back on and called his phone.

"Could you please take your ass home before you wake Prince up."

"Fuck that! Come open this door."

"I'm not opening the door. Why you didn't just stay where you was at? We ain't fucking with each other anymore. You ain't my dude," I said before hanging up and shutting my phone off.

Tank

"Tank, you hear me," she pushed me.

"All I hear is blah, blah, blah. Shut up, damn. I told your ass when you started giving me head that Nay was mine. Don't be upset when I go see 'bout her. You just a little side that ain't even got the dick yet. Ain't nothing more annoying than a female that don't know her place."

I was glad when I saw her grab her Fendi purse and leave. She was a local hairstylist that had just moved from Georgia. I wasn't really feeling her, but Nay was holding out on me and I need to release a few nuts, so I hemmed shorty up in the club one night. I told her all about Nay and Prince; she was cool with it. She even went through my photos and saw pictures of Nay; even saw some pictures she should not have seen, but hey. I needed some type of memory to jack to.

I was trying to make up an excuse to see Nay, but I couldn't think of one. I got dressed and headed to Persian's house. I hadn't spent time with the homie since Neek left. He'd been so busy with Shanice that he stayed low. Pulling up, I smiled when I saw Nay's car. I had no idea she was going to be here but shit; now I didn't have to come up with an excuse.

"What you doing here, bruh?" Persian looked over his shoulder.

"Shit, I was coming to chill with you. Rap about some shit."

"Nah, I don't think now is a good time. Nay here and she ain't really feeling you right now. As her big brother, I got to protect her.

Come back in a few though because she about to leave in a few."

"Damn, it's like that?"

"Give me fifteen minutes, bruh. Shit, I need a blunt and some Crown. All I've been doing is playing baby dolls with Shanice. I need some man talk. Bring your ass back," he yelled at my back.

"I got you, man."

I headed to the liquor store to get us some liquor and cigars. By the time I got back, Dre was there as well. Shit, we all needed a moment because our lives were jacked up.

"Dre, what's good with you my boy?" I dapped him up.

"Pour it up, man, we got a lot to talk about," Persian said. "Nay got Shanice and I need the blunts rolled up too."

We laughed and got drunk and high. It was just like it used to be, talking about our old ladies. Only person still had his woman was Dre. Persian and I were single as a dollar bill.

"Persian, how is Shanice holding up?" I asked.

"She cries every night. That shit hurts, bruh. I can't stand seeing her like that. She thinks her mama don't love her. If I ever see Neek I'm going to wring her neck, I swear."

"You still love her, don't you?" Dre asked.

"Hell yea! It pisses me off at times but my heart won't let her ass go."

"I feel you, bruh," I looked down at my watch.

I was enjoying my time with my boys but I was slick waiting on my baby to walk through that door. We ordered some takeout and was now playing Madden 17 when Nay walked in with the kids. She looked at me and rolled her eyes. The shit was sexy ass fuck as she walked upstairs with Shanice and Prince. I gave my controller to Dre as I headed that way.

"Don't make me come up there in put a bullet in your head 'bout my sister," Persian yelled.

I walked up the stairs and noticed she wasn't in Shanice's room because she was lying down for a nap. I walked down to the other bedroom and Prince was lying on the bed. I heard the toilet flush so I slipped in the room and locked the door. I walked in the bathroom while she washed her hands and jacked her maxi dress up.

"Tank, stop," she cried.

It was too late. I had already slipped inside of her. I melted as she gripped me. Looking at her in the mirror, I reached around and placed my hand around her neck as I softly stroked her.

"You been around him today, huh?" I glared at her reflection in the mirror.

"No!" she moaned.

"You lying! I smell that nigga's cologne on you. Does he do your body like I do?"

She gasped for air as I took myself out of her and spun her around so she could look me in my eyes. I sat her on the counter and let her slide down to her liking so I could enter her again.

"Answer me," I whispered in her ear.

"No."

"No, what?"

"He can't do my body like this," she said throwing her head back.

"You gave him my shit?" I gripped her neck again.

"No!"

That's all I wanted to know. We enjoyed our quickie before I cleaned up and headed back downstairs. I was relaxed like a muthafucka. Persian looked at me and shook his head.

"Your ass been up there so long Dre left."

"It wasn't that damn long."

"I hope y'all cleaned my shit up."

Nay came down the stairs with Prince. She must've heard us because her face was red.

"I'll come back to check on Shanice later this week," she said rushing out the door.

"Hell you be doing to her?" Persian raised his eyebrow.

I didn't respond. I ran out the door to catch her before she left.

"Nay! Hold up!" I jogged up to her.

"Tank, please stop this shit, okay? I'm sick of damn crying and shit because the man I want don't want me because he still likes to play little boy games."

"I'm not playing games. I'm here now! I'm sorry for being stupid but you know in your heart I don't want nobody but you. Let's stop playing games and start over," I begged.

"I can't."

"Why not?" she looked at her phone as it rung, displaying Mulik's name.

"It's because of him?" she couldn't even look at me and give me an answer.

"I won't hold you up. I'll hit you up for Prince," I backed away from the car and watched her pull off. Nay belonged to me and I was determined to prove it.

"Bruh, you got to work harder," Persian walked up behind me.

"She ain't feeling a nigga no more. I fucked up when I let old girl drive my shit. I swear I ain't slept with another woman since I hit Nay."

"Shit...you ain't got to sleep with a woman. You can just get some head and it's the same thing in women's eyes. Listen to me when I tell you. That's what messed my shit up. Now Neek got her ass in the Carolinas like I wouldn't find out where she was. We got to learn to keep it in our pants, bruh. Nay will come around."

"Not as long as that police sniffing up her ass," I stated.

"Who?" Persian leaned in to make sure he heard me right.

"Oh, she ain't told you she fucking with a fed?"

"I'm gon' fuck her up," Persian stormed off.

Nay had no idea the look she was portraying sleeping with the feds. All her street cred was being questioned.

Breya

"Shay, come help me with the food!" I yelled through the house.

She had been closed in her room all day and I wanted to know what was up. She had her days and I just gave her space. She walked in, still in her pajamas and hair in a messy ponytail.

"Did you at least wash your butt today? Talk to me, what's up."

She did the same shrug I used to do as a little girl. It was so much of me in her. Shay was beautiful but she didn't know it. She held her head down as she sat on the barstool.

"Shay, hold your head up. From this day forward, don't hold your head down anymore. You're beautiful and I hear your daddy tell you that all the time. What it's been, two weeks since you got your hair done?" I flipped her long ponytail.

"I think so."

"Go get dressed. The boys can find something for dinner. I'm gon' have to let you hang with me and Nay a little tighter."

"Hell no! Y'all not about to have my daughter around here learning how to shoot and pistol whip people," Dre stated, walking in the kitchen.

"Well, you and the boys need to find your own food. Shay and I about to go do girl shit."

After Shay got dressed, I took her to get a sew-in and then to get her feet and nails done. She deserved every bit of it. She was always doing for everyone in the house. We were now sitting down about to eat and I could tell something was bothering her.

"What's on your mind, Shay?" I poked at my food.

"I feel bad for what my mama did to you. I mean, I was looking forward to the baby and when you weren't around, my daddy was always worried. He really loves you and I'm glad you make him happy. That was something my mama never did. All she ever did was bitch—"

"Hey, watch it. I want you tough but with a clean mouth," I fussed.

"I'm sorry. All she did was fuss and beat us because daddy was with you or she was never there."

Listening to Shay talk brought back memories of my childhood; that's why it was so easy to connect with her because she was a little me.

"Well, don't feel sorry for what your mama did to me. I got to deal with these scars for the rest of my life but a bitch still fine," I stuck my tongue out.

Shay tensed up when a group of girls slid into the booth behind us. One of them I knew from the hood and she was a straight hoe. A few of the fellas ran through her and she was only in the twelfth grade.

"They be fucking with you at school?" I stared Shay in her eyes.

She shook her head yes. I couldn't stand a bully. Dre made sure Shay stayed on point and that's really what these lil' hoes was jealous of. After tonight though, that bully shit was ending. I slid out the booth since they wanted to giggle and be petty. Once I approached their table, all of them sat up except for the community hoe.

"Any of y'all got a problem with my daughter Shay?"

"Tell that hoe to stop talking to my nigga."

"Little bitch, don't I know you? A few of the fellas ran through your ass out on the south side," I told her. "And tell your nigga to leave her alone. I've been 'round when he called. Ain't he short with dreads and he got golds on his fangs? You ain't got to answer 'cause I know that's him."

She was on mute right along with her friends.

"Keep running 'round with her and all y'all gon' end up fucked up. Y'all need to dead that hating shit because next time I'll hire some girls to get in y'all shit," I said before walking off.

When I got back to our table, Shay was shocked. This was the person I needed her to be; she had to stand up for herself.

"What's that lil' bitch name because she never gave it to me."

"Lexus," Shay replied.

That was all I needed to know. And when I caught that nigga, I was going to check him too. I paid for our meals and we headed home. Dre texted and said him and the boys went out for pizza, so I was going to clean up while they were gone. This was never supposed to be my life. I was a tomboy at heart, but Dre changed that. I still laugh at how he hated how I dressed. I still wore my tennis shoes but I was a little more girly with it now. I was now standing in the mirror with a lace bra and panties, looking at my scars. Some days I couldn't look at myself. The keloids were never going anywhere. The scar on my chest and stomach bothered me more than the one on my face.

"You know you're still gorgeous, right?" Dre walked in the bathroom.

"Yea, I know. Sometimes I wish I would've done things differently, maybe my baby would still be here."

"Breya, stop beating yourself up about this shit. You're only twenty-seven, shit, we can try now for all I care."

I swear that's why I loved him. He wasn't into the whole dime piece look when it pertained to me. I was fine but I damn sure wasn't thick. I liked my men bigger than me and God must've known to make me little. Dre scooped me up and laid me on the bed. He climbed in and placed me on top of him. I laid my head on his slightly hairy chest. The rhythm of his heart soothed me as he rubbed my back.

"Breya, you know a nigga love you, right? You don't ever have to worry about me stepping out. I can't afford to lose what I have here with you and the kids. Shit, they finally got a home. I want to know will your little ass marry a nigga?"

I lifted my head up off his chest and looked at him. The same man I'd been messing with for years was asking me to marry him.

"Yes I'll marry you!"

"She said yes, y'all!" Dre yelled and the kids came running in excited.

"Damnit, Dre. I don't have clothes on," I punched him in the chest.

The boys brought the ring in and Shay followed behind them with a bigger box.

"What is this?"

"Open it," Dre demanded. I opened the big box and it was keys and a blueprint.

"Is this the blueprint to my dream house?"

"Yep! Now put this ring on."

"Alright kids, we love y'all, but y'all got to go!"

Nay

"Get comfortable," Mulik suggested.

I don't know what I was thinking coming over to his house. I was enjoying his company on our dates so I took him up on his offer to join him at his spot. I took my cardigan off and walked around looking at his art. He had great taste. I smiled at a picture of him as a little boy with braces. That was the magic behind his beautiful smile. He snuck up behind me and wrapped his arms around me.

"I wish I could have all of you but I can tell he still has a piece of you. I want to show you the other side of life. None of that street shit," he whispered in my ear.

I still hadn't slept with Mulik. I couldn't bring myself to do it. He was sexy and all that and I could tell he was working with something, but I just couldn't get Tank out of my mind. I spent as much time as I could with Mulik to keep my mind off of Tank. Sometimes it worked, sometimes it didn't.

"What is it about him that you love so much that you can't let go?" Mulik asked.

I really didn't want to answer that and hurt his ego, but Tank knew how to blow my back out and be rude all at the same time. I don't think Mulik was capable of being that thug in the bedroom like I so desperately needed. I was a thick girl so I needed that. Mulik was too much of a gentleman and that was okay, but just not what my body wanted or needed.

"I mean, I don't know. Tell me why you so pressed about him?"

"I'm not pressed, trust me. I just want your full attention when you are with me. I catch you sometimes gazing off and I know you're thinking about him. Tell me what I need to do to get you to focus on me."

"You're doing everything right. Just be patient with me, please."

"I don't know how much longer I can hold out around you," he rubbed himself against my ass. I walked away because I was not about to fall into his trap. He knew he was working with something and if he got me in the bed then he could change my mind. I wasn't crazy by a long shot.

"So what movies do you have?" I walked away into his den.

"It depends on what you want to watch. I'm not into the chick flicks but if that's what you into, then I guess I'll be a sucka for you," he laughed.

"Do I look like the type of girl to watch chick flicks? I need some murdering, drugs, and all that other hood shit," I stated.

Mulik went to pop us some popcorn while I took my shoes off and got comfortable. I could see us being friends but nothing more. He walked back in with his shirt off and my mouth hit the floor looking at his tribal tattoo, starting from his chest running down to the middle of his arm. I was glad when my phone started buzzing so I could take my eyes off of him. I ignored the text once I noticed it was Tank. He always tried to rain on my damn parade when I was with Mulik. I knew Prince was safe because Breya had him, so I didn't know why he was texting me. I decided to shut my phone off for the night and enjoy the rest of the night with Mulik.

"So you picked *Paid in Full*. Why is that?"

"Because I love this movie and this shit happens in real life," I replied.

"Humph."

I eyed him as he threw some popcorn in his mouth. I don't know what he was trying to imply but if he had some shit to be said, he needed to say what was on his mind. I enjoyed some of the movie before my eyes started getting heavy. I hadn't been sleeping a lot since Tank broke up with me. For one, I was still breastfeeding Prince and trying to sell my restaurant; and I just really missed Tank being in my bed. I stopped fighting my sleep and drifted off.

I woke up to the smell of sausages sizzling. I opened my eyes to see I was still in the same spot from last night with a comforter on. My clothes were still on and nothing was out of place. I stretched and went in the bathroom. Mulik had a toothbrush already out along with some toiletries and some clothes.

"He do this shit on the regular," I said as I turned the shower on.

I slipped into his basketball shorts and shirt before making my way into the kitchen. He had it all laid out with coffee and orange juice. He was really making it hard for me not to put a title on our friendship.

"Did you enjoy your shower?"

"Yes, I love that shower head. Why didn't you wake me up?"

"The way you were snoring last night, I didn't want to disrupt what the hell you had going on," he laughed. "Come on and eat because I know you gotta leave in a little while so I got to get as much of you as I can."

I gathered all my stuff after breakfast. I needed to pump because my breasts were huge. I was trying my best to wean Prince off the breast, but he was just as stubborn as Tank. You would really think he was his real father.

"I enjoyed you," Mulik said, walking me to the door. He left no room between us as he looked down at me. He lifted my chin and placed a kiss on my lips. I didn't stop him when I know I should have. He kissed me again, this time pushing his tongue into my mouth. I don't remember dropping my purse but some way, my hands ended up wrapped around him. Mulik started pulling at my shorts he let me borrow and again, I didn't stop him. He broke the kiss and stared at me.

"Come on," he picked me up bridal style and carried me to his room.

Here I was completely naked, lying in his king-sized bed, watching him strip naked. He was a god. His body was a woman's artwork. Once his briefs came off, I knew then this was going to be the last time I would ever see him again. He put a condom on and forced himself inside of me. He didn't do any of the things that Tank did to get me ready for his size. Mulik was doing so much grunting that it was turning me off. For the first time in my life, I felt like a hoe, and the sex was trash. A man with his size penis should know what to do with it. I was as dry as the Sahara desert and it was starting to hurt. I know Mulik felt it through his condom but he continued on, doing absolutely nothing. Ten minutes later, it was finally over.

"I better get going. I know Breya probably blowing my phone up,"

I said, getting dressed.

He laid there with the condom full of his semen. His panting was grossing me out. I didn't even give him time to walk me to the door. He did all that romance to end up being trash in the bed.

Tank

I sat in front of this nigga's house all night. I thought for sure Nay was going to come out but she never did last night. My WaWa Styrofoam cup was full of roaches from all the blunts I smoked. Here it was a little after ten in the morning and she was rushing out of his house. Muthafucka had her shoes in her hand. A nigga's heart was hurting. She was slipping through my damn fingers for this weak ass nigga. I wondered could I kill him and get away with it? I didn't really trust the nigga but Nay couldn't see it. I let her ass pull off as I continued to sit in front of his house. I wanted to see what his routine was. I needed to learn his ways so when it was time to catch him up; I had all my facts together.

I was drinking my fourth five-hour energy drink so I could stay up. The new Porsche I sat in blended in with the neighborhood well. I looked up to see him walking out the house with a little pep in his step. He fixed his tie before getting in his car. Pussy nigga don't even pay attention to his surroundings. I let his ass pull off. I waited about fifteen minutes to make sure he made it to I4 before I made my call.

"Aye, I need you and the crew to make some shit unlivable," I said into the phone.

"Whatever you need, Tank, just shoot me the address."

"Keep any shit that's valuable though," I said before ending our call.

I sent the text and pulled off. He wouldn't be sleeping peacefully tonight. That's what happened when you crossed boundaries. I picked up my phone out the cup holder when I saw Nay's face pop up.

"Fuck you want?" my voice dripped with hatred.

"Damn, fuck wrong with your dumb ass today?"

"Man, you called me, I didn't call you, so what you want?"

"I was calling to see if you was going to pick Prince up today. I need to go meet a potential buyer for the restaurant and I don't want to take him," she explained.

"Get him ready and I'll blow the horn when I'm outside," I said, and hung up in her face.

I don't know why I had an attitude with her, I just did. She had no business messing with him. My gut was telling me he had some shit up his sleeve and I was going to be on his ass when something popped off. I went home and changed cars because I didn't want Nay to know I bought a new car. It was really for her as a get back together gift, but she was playing with a nigga so I'll drive it myself.

I pulled up to her house and blew the horn. I noticed a for sale sign in front of her door. She was starting to really piss me off with all this secretive shit. She emerged out the door with Prince on her hip. He only had a few months before he turned one and I was going all out for my little man's birthday bash. I got out the car and opened the back door so I could put him in his seat. I loved our relationship. Every time he saw me, he just smiled. He was like my little buddy, and once he started talking, he was going to be hell.

"You selling your little ass spot?" I sarcastically asked.

"What the hell it look like, Tank? I'm buying another house. Prince is about to be one and I need a bigger spot so he can have room to run around and stuff like that."

Something was up with her. She kept her eyes down on the ground and not once did she look at me.

"You fucked him, didn't you?" I asked her.

"What?" she finally looked at me.

"Oh you heard me, but it's all good. I still love your nasty ass. I hope it was good to you because you'll never have this dick again," I got in my car and tried to closed the door.

"Don't you ever in your life call me nasty," Nay slapped the shit out of before storming off.

"Bring your ass here, Nay!" I yelled. "Don't make me snatch your ass, bring your ass here," my voice boomed.

She turned around and walked back to me with her arms folded across her chest.

"Look, I'm sorry for calling you nasty and shit. I'm gon' let your ass do you. You crossed the damn line with that shit right there. You broke all the damn street codes being with that nigga," I rubbed my hand over my face.

"Did I say I liked him? Maybe I like the way he treats me, did you ever think of that?"

I laughed, "You like the way he treats you? Muthafucka, you from the streets like me. All you like is thugs. It won't ever be another Tank, baby. It's only one me, and you'll never be able to fully move on from

Tank, baby," I cockily said. "Gon' and do you though, just don't try to hop back on my shit when he ain't handling you right."

I left her standing there as I pulled off, and just to piss her off even more, I blew a kiss and flicked my tongue at her. She stormed off, making her ass jiggle. The shit was funny to me. I was playing about my dick though. She could call me back right now and I'll knock her walls down.

"Hello?" I answered my ringing phone.

"Boss man, we got some shit you may want to see. Meet us at the pool hall."

See, even though Persian ended his side of the game, my shit didn't stop. I was doing shit before Persian brought me on. My pool hall with my uncle was the spot, including my clean-up crew, so the street life was just in me. I never took my son to the pool hall so I would have to drop him off to one of my crazy ass cousins for a few minutes so I could handle business.

I spoke to a few niggas before I headed down to the basement. There was a duffle bag sitting on the table. I looked at one of my clean-up boys and he nodded his head for me to open it up. I unzipped the bag and started pulling shit out. Once I had everything laid out, I rested on my elbows and looked at this shit in front of me. This Mulik fella was building his own damn case against me. It was never about Nay being arrested for distribution; this was a plan to get next to me and he got the closest thing to me to help him. Nay didn't even understand the shit she was in. She was sleeping with the enemy, if he took me down, then she could possibly go down too. The picture of the burned down house in Miami made my blood boil. He knew Nay killed that CO and he wasn't saying anything. This son of a bitch was trying to blackmail her to tell on me.

I took out all the cash I had in my pocket and gave it to my clean-up boy. This was some of the best information anybody had ever brought me.

"I don't need this, Tank. You take care of me very well," he said.

"Nah, fuck that. Take it as a bonus."

I put all the stuff back in the bag and headed to spend the day with my son. I'll deal with this shit when I didn't have my son with me.

Persian

"So you the muthafucka that's dating my sister?" I sat across from this pig with my arms crossed. I picked his name up off his desk. "Mulik Mitchell."

"Nice to meet you, Zyle," he held his hand out for me to shake it.

Once he saw that I wasn't here on no friendly shit, he sat his ass down in his chair. Even though I was on the other side of the desk, you could clearly see who the boss was from the way we stared each other down.

"Fuck you want with my sister? We don't really do feds because you can't be trusted. So tell me, what you want, money? I got plenty of it," I mugged his ass.

"I don't want money because I have my own. What's wrong with a decent brother just wanting to spend time with a girl like your sister?"

"For one, you knew my name before I told it to you so that means you been digging. Second, my sister ain't even your type. How long you been working for the feds?" I looked around his office.

"Many years… too many to count really."

"That's some strange shit though. You don't have any plaques on the wall for your service, no diplomas, and no pictures of your family. All you got is a whole bunch of damn papers to appear like you're busy. I've been in Orlando my whole life and I know almost the whole police force and majority of the feds because see, just like y'all study us street niggas, we study y'all too. I never heard of you though, Mulik Mitchell," I stared at him.

"You're a very observant man. I like that, but see, I've moved offices several times so most of my stuff is boxed up. An educated black man like myself moves up the corporate ladder, but you wouldn't know anything about moving up, would you?"

"Mulik, you're nothing but a fuck boy to me that did what his daddy wanted him to do. I'm the nigga that did what he had to do to feed his sister. My mama got murdered and left us at a young age. But see, you wouldn't know shit about that since you come from a six-figure home and went to the best private schools. I know some shit about you too and I know you're not from here. I don't know why I spent so much time talking to you because all I came to say is stay the fuck from 'round my sister," I stood up, knocking the chair down.

"If she don't want to stop fucking with me, what you gon' do?"

"Fuck with her and you'll find out," I laughed before walking out of his office.

Nay

I've taken at least three showers today while Prince was gone. I felt nasty as hell after I slept with Mulik. He had no idea but I was done with him. It was nice while it lasted. My day was so hectic. After negotiating for hours with a buyer of my restaurant, we finally came to an agreement we both liked. He couldn't believe how good I was with numbers. I was a woman about my business and I needed my coins. Now that the restaurant was off my hands, I could focus on opening up a clothing boutique which was really something I wanted to do anyway. The restaurant really haunted me and I lost my love for it.

I poured myself a glass of red wine as I waited for Tank to bring Prince back. I pumped enough milk to last him this week and we were done. He was entirely too big to still be on my breast. I enjoyed the moments of silence. I found time to catch up on my shows that I missed during the week. My phone was turned off and I was enjoying me time until my doorbell rang. I hated when Tank brought Prince back before it was time. I threw my throw off my legs and walked to the door. I looked through the peephole before I answered it. A frown came across my face.

"What are you doing here?" I asked Mulik. Stress was all over his face but I didn't give a fuck.

"My house fucked up, can I crash here?"

"What you mean your house fucked up?" I continued to stand to the door in my pajamas.

"Somebody broke in, trashed the place, and left all the water on so it flooded," he explained.

I stepped aside to let him in.

"That's fucked up. Don't take this the wrong way, but I can't let you stay here," I bluntly told him.

"Damn, it's like that?"

"I'm not being funny. I just don't let anybody stay with me. I try to keep my house safe for me and my son."

The doorbell rang again and this time I knew it was Tank. He was still early. This couldn't be happening to me right now. I was afraid Tank was going to flip once he saw Mulik in my house. I never once told Mulik where I stayed which was creepy. I went to open the door and Tank walked in with Prince reaching for me.

"What the hell he doing in here?" Tank stepped to Mulik.

"He was about to leave. Somebody fucked up his house so he stopped by," I explained quickly.

"Why the hell you telling him my business?" Mulik asked.

Shit, I don't know why I was explaining shit to Tank.

"Because that's what she supposed to do. You a stranger in this muthafucka, not me," Tank said.

"Y'all, please! Not in front of my son," I told them both.

"I'll leave. I'll call you tomorrow," Mulik said, bumping Tank on his shoulder.

Tank held up his trigger fingers at Mulik. I had started a big mess with these two. Mulik walked out, slamming the door. I don't know why he had an attitude; I didn't invite his ass over here.

"I better not ever in my life catch his ass back in a house I pay the damn bills in," Tank fussed.

I walked away from him, heading to Prince's room so I could get him ready for bed.

"Don't damn walk away from me."

"Tank, take your ass on now. Only reason I let you pay the bills in this muthafucka is because you begged me to. Don't play your damn self now. I can damn well handle my own. Now if you're going to argue like a little bitch about a nigga stopping by, then take your ass on," I said before vomit spewed out my mouth.

"You a nasty muthafucka. Can't even talk shit without throwing up and shit all over my son. Move your stankin' ass out the way so I can clean him up," he pushed me out the way.

I kept my mouth covered up as I continued to vomit, walking towards my bathroom. I knew why I was throwing up. I had already set up an appointment and no one knew, not even Breya. I cleaned everything up and brushed my teeth. Tank was bathing Prince so I decided to have another glass of wine just to try and act normal. I turned my shows back on and continued on like Tank wasn't in the house.

"You full of shit, Nay, I swear," he snatched the wine glass. "Let me find out you hiding some shit and you gon' wish you didn't. Only muthafuckas that throw up is a muthafucka carrying a baby."

"Tank, please leave me the fuck alone. I'm tired of arguing with your ass."

"I'm about to leave your ass alone but you heard what the hell I said. Oh, and keep that bitch away from here," he said before walking out the door.

***

The next morning, I couldn't sleep in because someone was banging on my door. I don't even remember Prince being in the bed with me, but he was sleeping peacefully on the other side of the bed. I slipped out of bed and went to the door, snatching it open before looking. Standing before me was Mulik. He was starting to step on my last nerve.

"What are you doing here, Mulik?" I leaned my head against the door.

"I need you," he tried to hug me.

I stopped him by placing my hand on his chest. It was time to break it down to him.

"Mulik, look. I don't think I can be friends with you anymore," I expressed.

"I guess your man got in your head?"

"No, that's not what happened," I was trying not to hurt his feelings and tell him that he was trash in the bedroom and couldn't compare to what Tank could do.

"Then what the fuck is it? I treat you good. I've given you all of me," he pushed his way in the house.

"Mulik, could you please just get out," I looked in the corner where my purse was, just in case I had to put one in his head.

"What the fuck you want from a nigga, Nay? You like thugs, huh? I guess that's why you like those gangsta ass movies. Let's not mention you have a different gun in your purse when you're with me. Oh! I checked. The numbers at your shoe store are doing good but it ain't bringing in enough for you to afford the different cars you drive."

"Are you fuckin' stalking me, Mulik?" I angrily asked.

"I know everything about you, I work for the feds. I also know you were the cause of CO Syriah's death."

I didn't show any emotion like he expected me to. I wasn't a pussy; he had to come with more than speculation.

"I have your attention now, don't I? Now, you're going to take your pretty ass in your bedroom and spread them pretty long legs, or I can call my boys in here to arrest you. Which would it be?" he eyed me.

I wanted to break down and cry. I wanted to grab my phone and call Tank so he could come save me.

"My son is in the bed," I told him, holding back my tears.

"Well looks like I'll take it right here then. Take all that shit off."

A tear rolled down my eye as I took my pajamas off. I thought about my son lying in the next room and I thought about the baby I was carrying. A man finally broke me down.

Persian

"That's good, Shanice," I cheered her and her team on.

I was finally getting the hang of this single father role. I had a surprise birthday party set up for her tomorrow. She gave me so much life. She had a lot of Neek's traits and I found myself getting emotional because I wondered what she was doing. I tried calling several times to at least check on my child, but the phone calls went unanswered.

"Your daughter has really stepped up for the younger girls," one of the parents said over my shoulder.

"Thank you," I replied. I pulled my ringing phone out of my pocket. The number was coming from Georgia. I didn't know anyone in Georgia so I ignored it, but they called right back.

"Yea," I said placing my finger over my ear so I could hear.

"Am I speaking with Zyle Maxwell?" a lady asked.

"Yes, who's speaking?"

"This is the charge nurse from Memorial Hospital in Savannah, Georgia. I was calling to let you know we have Aneeka Wilburn here and she's in labor. She's having a few complications that I can't talk about over the phone."

I hung up the phone in her face and got up off the bleachers, walking right in the middle of the girls dancing competition and snatched Shanice off the floor.

"Persian, is everything alright?" her coach ran up to me.

"Fuck no everything ain't alright. Neek's ass about to have the baby and I need to get there," I talked as she ran behind me.

I had banged her down twice since Neek been gone. I cut the shit off real quick though because she was getting attached too quickly. I turned around and glanced at her before walking out the gym with my daughter. Shit, she wasn't my girl so I didn't care about her looking sad.

"Daddy, is Neek about to have the baby?"

"Don't call your mama by her name. I've told you that before," I fussed.

"Yes, sir."

"Yes, she's about to have the baby and we need to get there, but it's far away. I know you've never been on a plane but we are about to get on one. Daddy going to make sure you're safe, aight?" I looked at her in the rearview mirror as she shook her head.

I pulled in to a parking spot at the airport. I checked to make sure I didn't have a gun or anything on me. I helped Shanice get out the car as we waited on the shuttle to take us to the gate. I prayed we could catch a flight at the last minute. I wanted to be there before she started pushing. The airport wasn't as packed as it usually was, which was a plus for me. After standing in line waiting for a flight, I was able to pay and catch a flight in the next hour. I called the hospital back to see if Neek was pushing. Once I found out she wasn't dilated fully, I relaxed a little more. I walked to get Shanice something to eat before we took off.

"Daddy, I'm scared," Shanice grabbed my arm.

I fastened her seatbelt and then mine before I wrapped my arms around her.

"You're going to be fine. Daddy won't let nothing happen to you. I'll die first before I let anything happen to you," I promised her.

The flight from Orlando to Savannah was smooth. I rented a car and headed to the hospital. Shanice and I got lost a few times before we were able to make it to the correct floor.

"Yes, I'm Zyle Maxwell and I'm here for Aneeka Wilburn," I told the nurse.

She started tapping at her keys before she looked up at me confused.

We don't have anyone here by that name, sir."

"Could you check again, please. I got a call from you almost three hours ago telling me she was in labor. I even called back and they said she wasn't dilated fully so I had time," I explained. I was trying not to get frustrated but it was getting harder by the minute.

"I don't see that name in here. I'm so sorry. Maybe I could get the charge nurse to talk to you."

"Yea, do that please," I counted to ten once I saw Shanice's big eyes looking up at me. I couldn't flip out on these people in front of her.

"Hey, I'm the charge nurse here. What's the problem?"

"I got a call from you stating that my girlfriend Aneeka Wilburn was here having a baby."

"No, sir, I didn't call you. Our floor is full and all of our mothers have had their babies. I'm very good with the names of my patients and she's not one of them. I could see if she's at the other hospital here," she suggested.

"Could you, please?"

I paced the floor holding Shanice's hand as the nurse called the other hospital.

"Sir, she's not there either. I'm sorry."

I pulled my phone out to show her the number.

"Did you call me from this number?"

"That's a Georgia number but it's not ours," she explained.

"Aight," I said walking away.

Somebody was fucking with me. My heart was racing because if Neek was in danger, I needed to know where she was. I got us a room for the night and booked our flight out for the next day.

***

"Can I go to auntie Nay's house, Daddy?" Shanice asked as we pulled back up to the house.

I was exhausted from the trip and stressed out. I needed Shanice by me until I figured some shit out.

"Not this week, baby girl."

She got out of the car and ran up to the door as I grabbed the Target bags out of the car. I couldn't let my baby girl go another day with her dancing uniform on, so I went and grabbed her some clothes while we were in Savannah.

"Daddy, what is this?"

"Don't touch that!" I dropped the stuff in my hands and jogged up to the door. It was a brown box with a red bow on it.

"Go stand by the car, Shanice," I yelled.

She took off running as I took out my gun and opened the box. I dropped the gun when I saw what was in the box. Tears streamed down my face as I took my shirt off and grabbed the baby girl out of the box. She was looking up at me with the placenta still attached to her. She looked just like me. This was too much for a nigga. I made sure she was wrapped up when I noticed the note under the red bow. I cuffed the bag in my arms as I opened the letter.

I hope you can take better care of her than I can. I love you!

Neek

Nay

*I*t's been two weeks since Mulik revealed to me that he knew I killed Syriah. It's also been two weeks since he'd been raping me. It started out once a day then he would pop up on his lunch breaks or call me all times of the night to come to his new place. He made sure to send me pictures of me and Breya in Miami. Me at the prison with Kevin and anything else he could send me to make me feel guilty. He had the warrant for arrest written up; all it was missing was the judge's signature. I felt like shit. I hadn't talked to nobody. I let myself go. I hadn't gotten a haircut. I hadn't answered the phone or door for anyone. I could barely take care of my son. He had started walking and my house was a mess. I was supposed to be out of this place and into my new place last week, but my energy was at zero. I missed my abortion appointment because I couldn't get away from Mulik to do anything.

"You got an hour to get over here. Make sure your son is sleep because I don't have time to sit around and wait on his ass to go to sleep," he said before hanging up.

I couldn't wait to slice his muthafuckin' throat. My hands were tied at the moment. If he had all this information on me, and he came up missing, then surely they were going to come to me because he made it his business to post pictures of me and the case all over his new house. So for right now, I had to do what I had to do to keep Breya and myself out of jail. I now know what Persian and Tank were trying to tell me.

I took a quick bath and got dressed. I decided to drop Prince off to Breya instead because he was nowhere near sleepy. I pulled up to her house and blew the horn. I turned the lights off in my car so she couldn't see me. I'd been avoiding her ass too, and I didn't need to be questioned right now.

"Nay, why the fuck you not answering my calls? Don't fuck playing with me either," she crossed her arms across her chest.

"Could you get your nephew out the car, pretty please?"

"When you bring your ass back I want damn answers. We better than this shit right here," she continued to fuss as she got him out the seat.

She closed the door and I pulled off before she could say anything else. I only had about ten minutes to make it and I was at least twenty minutes away. I cried all the way there. I cried because I didn't want to go, I cried because I should've listen to Tank, and I cried because there was nothing I could do.

"You're late! I was just about to call the judge. Don't play with me, Nay," he grabbed my jaws tightly.

I slapped his hand away and walked in the house, throwing my purse down, letting all the contents fall out.

"Come on and get this shit over with so I can go get my son," I spat.

"Humble yourself, bitch! I hate to see you behind bars because of your disrespectful mouth. As a matter fact, since you want to run your mouth, get on your knees."

I prayed this day wouldn't happen. I stood there and watched Mulik drop his underwear. The vomit that I was holding down was now making its way up my throat as I got on my knees.

"Don't be scared, he won't bite," Mulik laughed.

Mulik shoved his dick in my mouth, causing me to vomit everywhere. He hadn't cleaned himself and he tasted and smelled sour. He was doing shit out of spite; this was not the same Mulik that seduced me. Mulik picked me up by my neck and slammed my back against the corner of his table. The pain that shot down my leg was severe, but I ate it because I didn't want to be weak.

"Go get a washcloth and clean this shit up," he threw me to the floor.

I slowly got up and went to the bathroom to retrieve a washcloth.

"I don't even want none no more. Get the fuck out my house."

He made my day. I've been put out of better places. I picked up my purse and opened the door to walk out.

"I changed my mind. Bring your ass here right now."

I was tired of these games. I had to kill this muthafucka quick.

***

"Either a nigga fucking the dog shit out of you or he beating your ass. Which is it?" Breya sat in my bed.

"Damnit, I'm fine, just a little sore," I lied.

"You a damn lie! When we started keeping secrets?"

"Breya, trust me, I'm straight."

"Nay, you're not straight. You look like you've lost some weight. Your hair is a hot ass mess; you haven't packed yet. Oh, and I had to pay the got damn landlord to open the door and you in this bitch sitting in the dark. Do you have any idea what the hell is going on around you? Persian dealing with some major shit and you won't talk to nobody."

"Breya, you giving me a headache, bruh."

"Fuck it then! You call me when you ready to open your mouth. I'll stop by the shoe store and make sure they good. Nay, whatever it is that you going through can be handled, you just need to say the word."

After Breya left, I fixed me and Prince something to eat and started packing. There was nowhere in Orlando I could go without Mulik finding me. There was only one way out.

Tank

*H*earing the panic in Breya's voice scared me, and it reminded me that I hadn't talk to Nay in a few weeks. I was trying to stay away from her as I planned to kill her newfound love.

"Tank, do you hear me talking to you?" Breya yelled, getting my attention.

"Yea, I heard you. Meet me over there," I told her before hanging up.

I tried calling Nay but her phone was going straight to voicemail. I called Persian so he could meet us over there as well. I sat in front of Nay's spot until everyone pulled up. I didn't want to be alone with her. I smoked and just thought about her being pregnant; she couldn't even tell a nigga. She would rather keep entertaining ole boy. When she never spoke up, I let her ass go for good.

"Get your ass out the car," Breya tapped on the glass.

This nigga Persian was walking around this bitch with two little girls. He made me proud; he was handling that shit like a champ. I dapped him up as we walked up to the door. Breya used a key she paid to get made and unlocked the door. The house smelled good but shit was everywhere. This wasn't Nay. Prince was walking and I didn't even know it. He noticed us first and walked up to me with his arms out. I missed him like crazy. I kissed his jaw as he pointed to where his mama was. Nay sat on her floor crying as she packed. She never cried so whatever had her in this funk was getting to her. She was one of the strongest women I knew besides my mama.

"Ronaysha, what's up with you?" Persian stood over her.

She quickly wiped her face so we wouldn't see her. She looked up at me and held her head down. I rested my back against the wall and waited.

"You do hear me, right?"

"I hear you."

"Well you better damn answer me then. This shit got to stop, whatever it is. This bitch ass nigga you call yourself fucking with got you going against your family. I told your stupid ass to stop fucking with him and I stepped to his faggot ass too at his office a while back. Now you in this bitch avoiding the people that love you the most," Persian went off.

Nay broke down and it made me feel bad. I walked towards her and sat down on the floor and grabbed her. She melted as she cried on my shirt. This shit was deep; deeper than she was putting on for us.

"Baby, we can't help you if you don't tell us what's going on," I told her in her ear. No matter what, she was going to always be my baby.

Nay lifted her head as her phone rung. Persian went and picked it up to see Mulik's name on it.

"Aye, my man. I thought I made myself clear with you. Don't tear your ass with me, bitch. Don't call her phone no more and don't bring your ass here no more. And if you think I'm playing, just try me and I'll kill you on the spot. Bitch ass nigga," he said, throwing the phone.

"What the fuck he done?" Persian asked.

Nay looked around the room before she cleared her throat.

"He knows I killed Syriah in Miami so he's been blackmailing me. I have to be his sex slave whenever he calls," she broke down again.

Persian punched a hole in the wall. "Didn't I tell your ass to be careful? I knew some shit like this was going to happen."

While he continued to pace the floor, I got up and went to my car. This was just what I needed. I needed the team back together to eliminate our enemy. I was not about to let Nay go down without a fight. Him having sex with her was over. I walked back in the house with the duffle bag and dropped it in the middle of us.

"What is that?" Breya asked.

"This is what we need to take that nigga out. He got close to Nay so he could get to me. I didn't find that out until I found out Nay spent the night at his house one night, so I had my get em' boys go fuck his house up and they found this. Go head, take a look inside," I told them.

Persian pulled everything out of the bag and laid it out so everyone could see. The look on Nay and Breya's face showed anger.

"So this nigga had a plan just like I thought he did," Persian paced.

"I already got a plan but I need everyone in," I eyed them.

The room was silent but I could tell everyone was thinking. Breya spoke up first, followed by Persian. We all waited for Nay's response.

"What it's gon' be, Nay?" I asked her.

"I'm in."

"That's my girl," I slapped her ass.

Nay bonded with her niece while I went over the plan with them. My plan didn't involve Nay sleeping with his ass anymore, but I knew her shit was good so he was going to chase her before turning her in.

"So what's the plans for Neek?" Nay asked.

"As much as I love Neek, I ain't fucking with her like that no more. What kind of mother drops their baby off like that? Shit was uncalled for, fuck her. I'm focusing on Shanice and Aniya now. Now that you getting your shit together, I need help with these damn girls. I don't know shit about what girls go through. So when I call you, you better pick the damn phone up," Persian stated.

I laughed because it felt good to be around everyone again. I was waiting to get Nay by herself so we could talk. I had so much I wanted to say. She wouldn't be going through this shit if I wasn't acting stupid. I gave Persian the head nod when the girls weren't looking.

"Come on, it's getting late. Breya, you know you better get home before Dre comes busting his guns looking for you," Persian laughed.

"Wait, y'all ain't got to leave so early," Nay stated.

"You scared to be left alone with your nigga?" I mugged her.

"Never that," she replied.

"Well sit your ass down and let them people go home."

She sat back on the sofa as I walked them to the door. Once the door was closed, I walked back in the living room and took Prince off of her lap and placed him down so he could play with his toys. Nay busied herself with packing again. She was doing everything in her power to avoid me.

"Nay, bring your ass here and sit down."

She put the box down and came and sat on the sofa. Silence fell amongst us. I didn't want to say anything that was going to hurt her feelings, so I was trying to be careful.

"So how long you been pregnant? And don't lie to me either," I warned her.

"I'm probably about two months."

"So, when were you going to tell me?"

"I wasn't going to tell you. I was going to get rid of it," she said bluntly.

"I can't stand foul females that do dumb shit like that. I swear if I would've found out you did that shit I would've killed you. Does he know?"

"No! Why the fuck would I tell him?"

"Shit, I'm saying. You was going hard for that nigga."

"Tank, if you gon' talk down on me you can leave."

"I ain't going nowhere. You might as well leave this shit here and grab you and Prince's clothes and bring y'all ass to my crib."

"I'm not moving in your mama house with you, the hell I look like?" she rolled her eyes.

"You talk too damn much sometimes, I swear. Pack y'all shit and bring your ass on. You ain't talk to a nigga in a good minute, so you don't know where I lay my head."

I had a brand new spot ducked off from Orlando. I stayed there during the week and spent the weekends in my mama's crib so I could be close to my money. Nay would have known that if she was answering my calls.

Mulik

"Why am I still sitting in this piece of shit, Mulik?" Kevin added pressure to the crevice of my elbow. "You better not scream you little bitch," he gritted.

"Please, Kevin, I'm working, I promise," I pleaded.

"Only thing I heard you working is my baby mama. I gave you everything you asked me for. If I'm not out this bitch soon, I'm killing your whole family."

"Shit like this takes times. Nay ain't just an easy person to talk to," I explained.

"You want to know why? 'Cause you round here treating her like a damn slave instead of sticking to the plan of being a gentleman. I know her shit good; I can't wait to get back in it," I could tell he was sitting here thinking about Nay.

"I'll try to get back on her good side."

"Humph, it might be too late. Her and her brother are close and if you've been keeping her away from him, it won't be long before he figures this shit out. That's another reason you need to finish the paperwork to get me out of here."

"I'll finish it when I get back in the office," I promised.

I had no intentions on helping Kevin get out of prison. I did have some flaws in my report but only we knew about it. If I could get rid of Kevin then no one would ever know. I've always been the type of dude that most called crooked. I took pride in putting people away that posed a threat to me. I loved having Nay at my beck and call. As soon as I hit Orange County, I was going to call her and make her come fuck me in my detective car while I recorded. She was turning into my little dirty whore and I was about to rub it in Tank's face. Since I couldn't lock him up, I took the next best thing from him.

Three hours later, I was pulling in front of Nay's spot. I got rocked up just thinking about her bent over the back seat. I got out and adjusted myself as I knocked on her door. I walked around to the back to see if I could see inside the house. The patio door blinds were slightly open. Everything was still in place. I knew she was supposed to move but she was slow about doing it because she didn't want me to know where she was going. I pulled out my work phone to call her since her brother answered the phone the last time on that bullshit. Her voicemail came on so I got back in my car. I headed to Tank's side of town. I knew where his mama's house was and I knew he laid his head there.

"Hell you doing sniffing 'round my auntie's house?" a girl with a mouth full of golds walked up the sidewalk.

"Oh, I was looking for something," I lied, trying to walk back to my car.

"What the hell you looking for with your police ass? We don't play that shit over here. You better take your ass back across the bridge with that shit. You looking all in my cousin's car and shit. Get the fuck on before you go missing," she threatened.

"Don't threaten me, you may regret it," I told her.

"Oh yea, so will you, pussy," she lifted her shirt to reveal her strap.

I was way out of my area and I knew crossing over into the hood was a big step. I often cruised through in my car and Tank would be posted up, but that's all I would catch him doing.

I got back in my car and headed home. Once I got home, I was going crazy thinking about where Nay was. I got back in my car and headed to her spot again and she still wasn't there. I slowly rode by her shoe store but she wasn't there either. Something was telling me that her and Tank were together. My phone started ringing. I got excited thinking it was Nay returning my call.

"Where you been?" I said into the phone.

"Why? I've called your office and you haven't attempted to go in and sign that paperwork. You've been home for hours now. Mulik, I hate to fuck you up but you're taking me for a joke. I don't like to play games," Kevin said.

"I'm on the way to the office as we speak," I told him.

"You got thirty-six hours to get me out of here or your job and your family is dead," he hung the phone up in my face.

"Shit!" I hit the steering wheel over and over again. I was going to kill Nay when I caught her. I didn't want to arrest her; I really wanted Tank, but she wasn't giving him up very easily. My boss was going to think I was crazy once I pulled the report out on Kevin. I rushed to my office and shredded all the documents so when it came back to me, I would act like they were misplaced. I learned my lesson about partnering with a street nigga.

Tank

The smile that spread across Nay's face warmed a nigga on the inside. We both agreed to give our relationship a try but we both had to get tested for any sexually transmitted diseases. She promised me each time she slept with Mulik he used protection. I was glad to hear that, but I was a nigga, and I didn't like the fact that another nigga was in something that belonged to me.

"So you guys are use to this procedure. Let's see if we can find a heartbeat today," the doctor said.

I sat Prince on my leg and bounced him. We had his party scheduled for tomorrow at our new place, and Persian pulled out all the stops. No one had heard from Mulik which was weird, but I wasn't letting my guard down. I knew he was just plotting on his next move and we were equipped and ready.

"Strong heartbeat; that's what I like to hear. Now, you're still early in pregnancy so I won't see you again until about six weeks, but I'm just a phone call away."

"Thank you, doc," I told her.

We were settling down for the night. I laid Prince down in his bed and kissed him before making sure the camera was on in his room. I walked in our room and I could hear the shower going. I slipped out of my clothes and quietly walked into the bathroom. I missed Nay, and all I wanted to do was feel her. I walked into our shower. Wrapping my arms around her waist, I slowly moved my hands up to her breasts. I placed soft kisses on the tattoo that traced her spine. I kissed both of her cheeks before I placed her knees on the bench that I had built in the shower. Spreading her legs, I latched on to her clit. Hearing her gasp was the encouragement I needed. I knew she missed me as much as I missed her ass. My dick was so hard it was hurting. I made sure she got an orgasm before I got up.

"Come here," I looked at her with squinted eyes.

She got up off of her knees and came towards me.

"Place your arms around my neck."

She wrapped her hands around my neck as I picked her up and slid her down on my dick. I sucked on her neck as she rolled her hips. I turned the water off and walked her to the closet where I sat down on the chaise and let her ride me until her insides spilled all over me.

"Damn, you dripping all on a nigga. Get your big ass up and put that ass in the air. I want to see that shit while I'm cumming."

Nay did just what I asked. I bent down and kissed her ear.

"I ain't going nowhere. I love your ass," I whispered.

"I love you too, baby."

That's all I needed to hear before I released inside of her.

"Can a nigga get a meal?"

"Really, Tank?"

"Hell yea for real. I'm tired as hell."

"It's late as hell. What you want me to cook?"

"Shit, make me egg and cheese sandwich."

I laid my head back and closed my eyes. A nigga got his family back. Now to get rid of Mulik before he destroyed what Nay and I built.

***

"Happy birthday, Prince," Nay sang. We decided to have the party at Persian's house because I didn't want anyone to know where Nay was. I was supposed to be enjoying myself, but my trigger finger was itching like a muthafucka so I kept my head on swivel.

"You need to relax," Nay said, kissing my lips.

"I'm straight, baby. Just keep your eyes open. Some shit ain't feeling right," I popped her on her ass and she went on about her business. My phone vibrated in my pocket.

"Talk to me," I said walking off.

"Feds busted in your mama's house, bruh."

"Keep an eye on their ass, I'm on the way. It's clean but I don't trust they ass."

I walked up to Nay to tell her where I was going.

"You straight, bruh?" Dre asked.

"The boys at my ma dukes house. I know it's Mulik's ass."

By the time I pulled up, they were still there plundering through my cars. The shit was funny to me. I was young but far from dumb. The hell I look like keeping shit over here. I politely walked up to the front door and entered.

"Can I see the warrant?"

They all looked up at me like I was speaking Chinese.

"Yea, the warrant. Where's it at?" I eyed them.

"Y'all give us a second," I heard Mulik's voice behind me.

"But you told us—"

"Give us a got damn second!" he yelled.

Standing in the presence of this pig was the hardest thing I've ever done. All I could envision was beating his ass and sticking my gun down his throat before pulling the trigger.

"Where is she?"

"She who?" I laughed.

I watched as he tightened his fist.

"Where is Nay?"

"Bitch, you got some nerve asking me 'bout where my girl at," I laughed again.

"I don't find shit funny here."

"Of course you wouldn't. You're the one that has to go back to your supervisor and explain that you came up empty-handed," I stated.

"Trust me when I tell you, I'll have your head on a platter. I can't stand young thugs like you walking around thinking your shit don't stink."

"I'll die before I let you have me, pussy nigga. Now, you and your boys get the fuck off my property before the sun goes down and it turns into something you not ready for."

Mulik shook his head, "We will see how hood you are when I catch you slipping."

"Why you still talking to me?" I mugged his ass.

When they left, I paid a few folks to come in and clean up the mess they left. I could've easily called Mulik in since he never showed me a warrant, but what real street nigga would do that? By the time I made it back to Persian's place, everyone was gone. Breya, Nay and Shay were cleaning up while Persian and Dre babysat the kids.

"Everything cool?" Persian asked.

"You already know who and what it was. His days are numbered though."

"The plan is still a go, he just hasn't grabbed the bait," Persian stated.

"He will, trust me."

"We got everything cleaned up. We're about to head out before the sky falls," Nay entered the den.

As soon as she got the words out, the rain came down.

"Damn, Shanice hates the rain," Persian expressed.

"I'll go talk to her," Nay stated, walking off.

The doorbell rung and all three of us went for our guns.

"Fuck is that coming over in a storm?" I eyed Persian.

"I guess we 'bout to find out."

The way things were going with Mulik, I followed Persian to the door. If some shit popped off, I needed to have his back. Persian cocked his pistol and opened the door, aiming the gun at the person on the other side of the door. The sight before our eyes was horrifying.

Neek

"Persian, baby, help me, please!" I stood in front of them soaking wet.

I took a big chance coming back here but I was running for my life once again and Persian would always be the one I run back to. I held my head up and looked him in his eyes. I could still see the love he had for me that would never die. We shared something that he didn't have with any other female. We shared two daughters.

"Y'all help me get her in the guest room before Shanice sees her ass," Persian picked me up.

I knew he was disappointed in me. I was young and dumb. I had everything I needed here with him, but I ran like the little girl I was. Tank didn't even budge to help me. He could be so hateful at times, and then turn around and be nice.

Behind closed doors, Persian stripped me out of my clothes and ran a hot bath. I knew he wasn't going to let me lay in his expensive sheets with my odor. He helped me in the tub and no words were spoken between us. He held a mug on his face as he washed my body. I was so tired but to hear my daughter's voice perked me up a little.

"How are my babies?" I asked.

"You don't have the right to ask me shit. The only reason I'm even helping you is because of them. I'll let them see you when I'm ready to. You're not about to keep popping in and out of their lives and shit," he spat. "It's some of your old shit on the bed when you ready to get out. Don't come out this room until my kids are sleep."

I leaned back in the vintage tub as he walked away. I loved when Persian wore wife beaters. His back muscles flexed as he walked away. I finished bathing and got out the tub. I was in desperate need of sleep, so I doubted Persian or the kids would know I was here. Stepping out of the tub, I could hear Nay talk to my daughter. Hearing Shanice talking about hating me hurt my feelings. How could she love Persian and Nay more than she loved me? I birthed her and took care of her while I took beatings from her sorry ass daddy. Even when Persian came along, I took care of her while he was in the streets making money. A wave of thunder hit and Shanice screamed. She always was scared of thunder and rain. She started being scared of thunderstorms one night her daddy beat me so bad that he threw us out in the rain for the night.

I finished drying off and put the clothes on that Persian had laid out, before I climbed in bed. I tossed and turned thinking of a way to get things back to how they were. I would never tell Persian that I snorted powder and took a few shot of heroine to ease my pain. He thought I was in the Carolina's but I was really here in Orlando with the love of my life. I finally fell asleep but I could feel someone standing over me. I rubbed my eyes to see Persian standing over me mugging.

"Why you standing over me like that?"

"What the hell you want, Neek? You want money? I don't need you fucking up my peace. I finally got the girls where they need to be. This shit you doing gon' mess Shanice up. Aniya don't even know who the hell you are and I really don't want her to. What kind of mother

140

calls to get me distracted just so she can drop the baby off on my doorstep? Neek, you ain't shit and you ain't gon' never be shit for what you've done to us."

"I'm so sorry, Persian," I cried.

"Suck that shit up. I been holding this in for a lil' minute. Them tears don't mean shit compared to the tears Shanice cried. It took months to get that girl to sleep in her room because she thought I was going to leave her too. I want your ass out my shit in the morning. All you can say is you're sorry. I don't know where your ass coming from and what kind of pressure you bringing to my spot. Wherever you come from, take your ass back," he finished.

"Persian, I need your help."

"You always need my help. This time, though, I can't help your ass. I'm looking at the big picture here and that's those two girls in there. So in the morning, get off your ass and get out," he walked out.

***

The next morning, I was up and ready to leave. I made sure my face was washed and teeth were brushed before I headed downstairs. As I waltzed down the stairs like the queen I was, Persian yanked me by my Nike shirt.

"You think you real damn slick. You bring your monkey ass down here after you knew the kids were up."

"You told me to leave this morning. Your ass didn't say what time," I smiled.

"Daddy, Aniya crying," Shanice came around the corner.

Persian let my shirt go and tried to block me from seeing my daughter.

"Hey, Shanice," I said in a high pitch voice.

"Mommy?" she looked at her daddy for reassurance.

"Come here. It's me. I'm back, baby," I grabbed her and hugged her. Persian looked at me with hatred in his eyes as he went to check on Aniya.

Got his ass, I thought as I hugged on Shanice.

Nay

I was finally able to get back to work. Two months had passed and Mulik finally got the picture to leave me alone. He had a big write up in the paper about some bogus cases, but he didn't get any jail time because of his father, who was an old judge. I didn't give a fuck one way or another. I let that small part of my life slip to the back of my head. Mulik was a distant memory.

I sat on my computer ordering the latest clothes and shoes to put in my newest boutique. I was giving the town something to talk about. I hadn't revealed the location to anyone. I didn't plan on opening until after the birth of my daughter, but I was a control freak so I wanted everything in place. A reminder popped up on my screen to pick out bridesmaid's dresses for Breya's wedding. I picked my phone up to call her.

"Bitch, I was about to come up there and fuck you up, you better be lucky you called me. You know damn well I don't know shit about being a damn girly girl."

"Breya, didn't I tell you I got you? You know I have to set reminders. I'm about to finish up what I'm doing and I'm going to go talk with one of the girls that makes my jeans. She got some hot designs that I'm going to look at for you."

"Thank goodness somebody got a sense of style. Call me when you leave and I'll meet you," Breya said.

"Ok, I will."

We talked about a little bit of everything before we finally hung up. I sent a text to Tank to meet me for a quickie before I headed to the designer. I was obsessed with Tank. I was afraid that if I didn't get myself together I was going to hurt someone over him. The girls were just coming back from lunch, so I slipped out the door to get in the truck with Tank.

"Your lil' nasty self couldn't wait until we got home?" Tank kissed me.

"It's mine, right?"

"You damn right."

"Well shut up and give me my dick."

Forty-five minutes later, we were out of breath and sweating in the hot Orlando sun. Sex between us was amazing. Nobody could do me like Tank could and vice versa. Our love was real and everyone around us knew it.

"Now that you've spent your lunch in here with me, what you gon' feed my daughter?"

"Just bring me something back," I told him, adjusting my clothes.

"Alright, I get to go get Persian first. He called me and said none of his cars would start. Of course, he thinks Neek's sneaky ass done something."

"He always thinks she's up to something since she got back. She ain't did shit but sat in that house and took care of the kids to give him a break. I'm gon' check him about that shit when you bring my food," I told Tank, putting my heels back on.

"I'm gon' need you to chill with them heels too. Ain't nothing wrong with wearing some damn flats. Your big head ass fuck around and fall and hurt my baby, I'm slapping the shit out of you."

"Shut up. Give me a kiss," I kissed all over his cute face.

"I'll be back," Tank said once I got out the car.

By the time I made it back inside, the store was full of customers. I greeted some of them before working the register a little bit. It had been two hours and Tank still hadn't brought my food. I waited until everything slowed down before I slipped in my office to call him.

"Hey, Nay," Neek walked in before I could dial the number.

"Girl, what you doing way over here on this side?" she looked better than she did two months ago. She had gained a little of her weight back and her hair was healthy again. Persian wasn't fucking with her like that. He mostly stayed at my house just to stay away from her. I noticed she didn't have the kids with her, which was strange if Persian was with Tank.

"Umm, Neek, where are the kids?"

"They home. A girl can't come and chill with her big sister for a little while? All I do is sit in that damn house with them kids," she complained.

"Well if you're here with me, is Persian home with them?" I asked.

"The kids are fine, Nay," she sat across from me, but she was antsy.

"So what is it that you want to talk about?" I powered on my laptop.

Neek looked at her nails and finally at me. She just stared at me for a minute. She crossed her legs and ran her fingers through her long hair.

"I never told you this but, I really looked up to you until you betrayed me."

"What the fuck you mean betrayed you?" I asked, pissed off.

"Let me damn talk, Nay. I rode for your ass hard. I thought you were one of the baddest bitches walking in Orange County. Everybody wanted to be Ronaysha Maxwell, even little me. Where you fucked up with me, was when you started fucking with Shanice's daddy."

"Now you pissing me off. I've only slept with two men willingly; a hoe is something I've never been. Shanice's daddy dead anyway, bitch. My brother made sure of that. Furthermore, why you checking me about some dick that's probably community dick anyway."

"Bitch!" Neek slammed her small palm on my desk.

"Calm that shit down, Neek. You know firsthand I'm not with the shits. I'll forget you was once my brother's girl and mop my marble floors with you," I stated.

"Calm down, baby." Mulik walked in the door placing a kiss on Neek's lips.

This was some real life soap opera shit. Nigga made me sick.

"So you the bitch ass nigga she in here checking me about?" I laughed. "How the fuck you get in here? I told my staff to never let you in here again."

I turned my camera on to see my staff laid out on the floor. Neek coming back home was a set up. Mulik knew the only way to get close to me was through Neek and she was too blind to see he was using her too. I reached under my desk where I had two glocks strapped to the desk and pulled them out, aiming one at Mulik and one at Neek. He pulled his out at me and Neek was left in the open with nothing.

"Y'all some dumb bitches for real. What type of nigga you got here that won't make sure you strapped? So since he's Shanice's daddy, who you had my brother kill?" I tapped the trigger lightly.

"My pimp," Neek looked at Mulik quickly before looking back at me.

Mulik shot her in the side of the head before he put the gun back on me. Neek's body hit the floor as thick dark blood spilled from head. I placed both guns on him. One center mass and the other right in between his eyes.

"She was a dumb bitch anyway. I hate your brother and she would never give me access to him. Good riddance, bitch," he looked at her dead body.

"I promise if I let off the first shot I won't miss," I told him.

"Big bad ass Ronaysha Maxwell. It's good to know I know what that pussy feel like. Kevin told me it was good and boy was he right," Mulik laughed.

"What you want from me, Mulik?" I held my position.

"I want Tank," he replied.

"I'm here, pussy nigga," Tank walked in with his gun trained on Mulik.

I was so glad to finally see him walk through the door. Only person missing was Persian. I knew he would've loved to see Neek's blood spilling on my floor.

"Ahhhh shit, now we talking," Mulik laughed.

"You one gun short, homie. My girl got two and I got two. It's only one of us walking out this bitch dead," Tank stated.

"You right, somebody not gon' make it out this bitch. I ain't got shit to lose," Mulik confirmed.

"I'm tired of him talking," I squeezed both my guns. Mulik's head snapped back and he fell over the chair and hit the floor.

"Your guns registered?" Tank asked.

"I'm good, you good?"

"Always, baby," he kissed me.

"Police on the way, I hear the sirens. I got some shit in the car, so I got to leave before they get here. I'll see you at the house," Tank stated.

The phone on my desk started ringing. I looked at Tank and shrugged. I answered it to see who it was.

"Baby mama, did you miss me? I'm on the way to get my son, bitch!" Kevin laughed before hanging up.

TO BE CONTINUED

Looking for a publishing home?

Royalty Publishing House, Where the Royals reside, is accepting submissions for writers in the urban fiction genre. If you're interested, submit the first 3-4 chapters with your synopsis to submissions@royaltypublishinghouse.com.

Check out our website for more information:

www.royaltypublishinghouse.com.

Text ROYALTY to 42828 to join our mailing list!

To submit a manuscript for our review, email us at submissions@royaltypublishinghouse.com

Text RPHCHRISTIAN to 22828 for our CHRISTIAN ROMANCE novels!

Text RPHROMANCE to 22828 for our INTERRACIAL ROMANCE novels!

Do You Like CELEBRITY GOSSIP?

Check Out QUEEN DYNASTY!
Visit Our Site: www.thequeendynasty.com

Get LiT!

Download the LiTeReader app today and enjoy exclusive

content, free books, and more

CPSIA information can be obtained
at www.ICGtesting.com
Printed in the USA
LVOW13s1020100317

526787LV00009B/132/P